I0451691

Once and For All

Bon Chance Boonies

A. L. Vincent

Published by Bienvenue Press, 2020.

This is a work of fiction. Similarities to real people, places, or events are entirely coincidental.

ONCE AND FOR ALL

First edition. August 11, 2020.

This book is dedicated to the people of D.J's, The Bar, and Legends. Carly's story really began then through conversations, experiences, and support. There are way too many to be named, and I'm sure that there are some that would rather remain nameless. Just know that I appreciate you all. You are the original "Boonies".

Also, I would like to give special recognition to a favorite daytime regular who has now since passed:

RIP Mr. Larry (Top)

Semper Fi.

Chapter One

••••

Carly Devereaux rolled over in bed, one eye opening to see the time on the clock on her nightstand.

The red light shone 10:00 a.m.

She groaned and started to get up. Sammy, her fat and ancient weenie dog, thumped a heavy tail under the blankets. Probably hoping to get another half hour or day of sleep.

Carly pulled the sheets back. "Come on, lazy. We have to get up. We have a party to get ready for."

Carly managed Snapper's, the bar and grill she owned with her brother, Noah, and best friend, Joey. They had opened it a couple of years ago, after their younger brother, Benjamin, had been killed in an oilfield accident.

Tonight was a big birthday party for Tessa, one of the bar's regulars, and Carly needed to be there to make sure everything was ready. She had already decorated, but there were a few last-minute things to take care of. Jell-O shots to make. Extra beer to stock. The food, her roommate Joey would make. She was a hot mess in the kitchen. But Carly would need to make sure there was adequate plates, silverware, and Jell-O shots.

As she thought about food, she smelled bacon cooking. Her stomach growled. Sammy, who was still half under the blankets, flopped around and stood up.

Carly laughed and patted her on the head, "Yeah, that bacon gets you going every time, doesn't it?"

A hearty ear flop was her answer.

Carly picked the dog up and placed her on the floor. She did a little dance around Carly's legs as they walked to the door.

The tip-taps of the dog's feet accompanied Carly's footsteps as she headed through the house she and Joey had shared since she returned from Biloxi.

She reached the open kitchen that Joey and Noah had remodeled recently, and her heart started doing that weird flutter thing it had been doing for the past few months.

Joey was at the stove wearing pajama pants. His hips swayed slightly to the Cajun music playing on the streaming radio station. His dark hair was rumpled. When he turned and flashed that dimpled smile at her, she had to look away to keep from throwing herself in his arms.

Instead, she crossed the kitchen and poured herself a cup of coffee.

Sammy, that bitch, trotted over to Joey and placed a paw on his bare foot. She rolled over on her back, kicking her tiny legs up in the air. She was rewarded with a tummy rub and piece of bacon.

"Sammy, let's go out," Carly said as she opened the door, and the dog pranced out. She plopped down on the bottom step while Sammy sniffed around the grass.

Carly couldn't see the water from where they were, but it was a short walk she made often.

"C'mon, Sammy," she said, and the little dog took off, ready to go on an adventure.

Reaching the beach, Carly sat, her coffee mug still in hand. She continued to sip while Sammy wandered along the water's edge, nose to the sand, looking for something. Carly had long ceased wondering what the dog was on the hunt for.

The heavy clouds were shades of gray and navy blue. It was hard to see where the clouds ended and the water began. White surf churned and splashed against the sand.

A storm was brewing.

Carly frowned and took a sip of her coffee. A cold breeze blew off the water, and she shivered.

She thought of Joey and her reaction to him in the kitchen. The same feelings she'd been fighting for months now.

The ocean wasn't the only thing in turmoil.

• • • •

JOEY FROWNED AS HE watched the door slide close behind Carly. Things hadn't been the same between them in months. She didn't grab him to dance anymore. She seemed distracted and was drinking more than usual. She was unhappy about something and wouldn't tell him why. Carly had always told him everything. This distance had his stomach in knots. He wondered what he had done wrong. He had considered talking to Noah or their other friend, Ryder, about it, in case she had said something to them, but had never asked. He kept hoping it was just a phase, that she would snap out of it. But so far, she hadn't.

He placed the last of the bacon on a paper plate and poured another cup of coffee. He leaned against the kitchen counter. He sipped his coffee and thought of her coming out of the bedroom that morning, her blonde hair a mess and brown eyes still heavy lidded from sleep.

He wanted so much to take the few steps that separated them and gather her into his arms, to feel her body pressed against his. But he couldn't do it.

They seemed to have reached an impasse. He had been friends with Carly too long to not be able to read her like a book. He could see in her eyes that she wanted him. He could also see the fear.

And it was the fear that kept him from acting on what he knew they both wanted. Carly ran when she was scared or hurt, and Joey couldn't bear it if she ran away from him.

The glass door slid open again. Sammy and Carly were back. Carly poured another cup of coffee and sat at the bar.

"Still really no idea where the storm is heading?" she asked, gesturing at the TV where a weathercaster stood in front of a map, pointing to a blob of green.

"Nah, you know how it is. They have all kinds of models and whatnot, but it's still just a tropical depression somewhere around Jamaica."

"Oh, good."

"I'm thinking I may head out tomorrow and pick up a few things, just in case. We're off tomorrow, and it's best to beat the rush. You know how it gets. You can't find water, bread, or ice anywhere if you wait too long."

"That's a good idea."

"Want to come with?" he asked, hoping she'd say yes. "We can stop at that Mexican place you like. The one with the two-for-one margaritas."

She smiled. "Maybe."

Her smile twisted his insides and made him look away. He was a chicken. He was scared, plain and simple.

Yes, they might work out. But the fear they wouldn't and that everything would change was too big. Joey couldn't risk losing her on a maybe.

• • • •

CARLY OPENED THE DOORS to the bar to allow the breeze to blow in. It helped to clear out the overall musty smell of the old wooden building and the stale odor of cigarettes and beer. Coming back in, she turned on the weather channel. The weather forecasters had been talking about a disturbance in the Gulf, and she wanted to stay updated on the situation.

She walked through the small, dark bar, making sure the tables were wiped down, the ashtrays were set out, and everything was the way it should be. As she did, she turned on the neon beer signs hanging on the walls.

Her favorite crowd, the daytime regulars, were mostly retired fishermen and oilfield workers. They were hard-working men who loved to get together for a few beers and some conversation. Carly never had any idea where their discussions would lead. It could be sex, sports, politics, or the weather. Most of the time, it was sports and weather. Today, with the storm, it would be the latter. Where did they think the storm was headed, how bad would it be, and most importantly, would they evacuate?

Would she evacuate? Where would she go? Every time a storm formed in the Gulf, Carly was plagued with these questions. This was home. Her comfort zone. To leave filled her with anxiety. And what about Sammy?

Carly turned off the TV and played the jukebox. Such thoughts would get her nowhere. In South Louisiana, tropical storms and false alarms were the norm.

She was finishing stocking for the day when her first regular came in.

"Hey, pretty girl," Daniel said, taking a seat at the bar. He was usually one of the first to come in. He would go have a late breakfast at the Redbird Inn with Glinda, read the newspaper there, and then make his way to Snapper's. Carly poured him a Coke and sat it in front of him.

"Hey, Daniel. How's it going?"

"It's going. And you? Getting any writing done?"

Carly frowned. "No. I'm stuck, Daniel. I just sit and stare at the empty page. Nothing is coming to me."

"Have you thought about working on something else for a while?"

"No. I'm just not feeling it. I think I've lost my mojo."

He smiled. "It will come back. Maybe you just need a break."

"I definitely need a break."

"Why don't you take a little vacation? Get away for a little while? That might get your gears going."

"Maybe. I have too much stuff going on with this place right now. We're celebrating Tessa's birthday tonight. After that, it's time to get ready for Halloween. That's just around the corner. You know how much I love Halloween. All the decorations, the costumes."

"It's a month away, Carly. Surely you can find some time to escape. Maybe take Joey with you. He could probably use the time off too. He's always busy in that kitchen."

"No!" She panicked at the thought of her and Joey somewhere alone. Her voice rose higher than she intended.

Daniel's eyes widened. "Something wrong between you two? You having one of your little spats?"

"No, nothing like that," she said, tempted to tell him everything, to lay it on the table. Another customer walked in, and she changed her mind. It would have to wait for another day.

• • • •

CARLY HAD JUST SETTLED on a bar stool when Ryder strutted in. "Still sitting here waiting for Mr. Right?" he asked. Grinning, he wrapped his arms around her and kissed her on the forehead. When she leaned back, she admired his long legs clad in black denim. He wore a belt buckle from a rodeo win, a black cowboy hat, and his irresistible smile.

"Shut up, Ryder," Carly said, smiling. "You know the answer to that. It wasn't that long ago that I thought you were my Mr. Right."

She was referring to when she initially began documenting her hunt for Mr. Right. Ryder's flirtatious nature had made her wonder if there was more than friendship, and after a few humorous attempts at picking him up, she had realized the truth.

He grinned and pulled her close. "Aren't you glad you were wrong?"

Carly leaned forward and put her head on his chest. "I've missed you. I'm glad you were able to come in this weekend. Still leaving tomorrow?"

"Yeah, have to get back to work."

Carly frowned. "How do you like Houston?"

"I hate it. The traffic sucks. Everyone always in a hurry to get somewhere. They'll run you over if you let them."

"Oh, and I'm sure you just hate that. I've ridden with you before," Carly said. Ryder had come to her rescue many years ago when she had gotten in a wreck in another town and was stuck. Riding with Ryder had been as scary as getting hit by a dump truck. He drove the same way he lived life, fearlessly and fast. Fast cars, fast bulls, fast women. That was Ryder.

"They do have a cool rodeo every year, though," he said. "I do enjoy that."

"I'm sure you do."

"You should come see me. Get away from this place. See some of the world."

"I've been in Houston before. Trust me, I know what I'm missing." Carly had lived just outside of Houston in League City right after she had graduated from college. She and her boyfriend at the time had moved there when she had gotten a job with Hilton Hotels. She had ended up leaving after coming home one too many times to a house full of high wanna-be musicians.

She sighed. "I would like to see Galveston again, though. That's a cool town. I hear they have awesome ghost tours."

"Come see me, then."

"I can't leave here. This place would fall apart," she said, waving a hand around her. Carly, Joey, and Noah had remodeled the old bait shop a few years ago and made it into Snapper's Bar and Grill. Snapper's in honor of Benjamin. Noah was the handyman, Joey cooked, and Carly managed the bar.

"I'm quite sure this place will be fine without you for a few days."

"I don't know."

"Carly, the only thing keeping you here is yourself."

"What do you mean by that?"

"Do you not trust your bartenders?"

"Of course, I do. My bartenders are awesome," she said. Several of them had been with the bar since it opened.

"They don't do their jobs?"

"They do."

"So, what is it?"

Instead of answering, Carly waved to the bartender. "Can we get a round of shots?"

"That's right, Carly, avoid the question."

"I don't want to think about it right now. It's Saturday night. You're here one more day." She batted her eyes at Ryder. "After all, tomorrow is another day."

"Yeah, I got your tomorrow," Ryder said. He took the shot glass from the bartender, and they clinked them together.

Carly cast a glance around the bar, her gaze landing on a picture from a few years before.

"What are you thinking about?" Ryder asked.

"I was thinking of that last Christmas we were all together. The New Year's Eve party. The one where Joey brought me my shoe after you threw it in the parking lot. Like he was some Prince Charming or something." Carly smiled. "Like he could even ride a horse."

"I remember that New Year's Eve."

"Lots has changed since that night. Noah came back, and so did Emily. They're together and doing well. Gabe and Grace are doing awesome. And this place..." she motioned with her head, "it's doing well. Look how the crowd is gathering already."

"Everything changes, Carly."

She looked to the back wall that held pictures from the past. "Yeah, seems that way..."

Ryder reached out a finger and tilted her head toward him. "Hey, now. This is my last night here. Don't make me go find someone to swing you around the dance floor."

"Save us both the embarrassment."

He spun on the stool, his long legs whipping around. He stood and shoved his black cowboy hat on her head.

"You never know. It is Saturday night. And I know where I want to end up."

"Well, good luck with that," Carly said. With his charm and those dark good looks of his, he probably would end up in some pretty young thing's bed.

"You never know, Carly. You never know who might walk in that door next."

As if on cue, the door swung open. Carly's mouth dropped, and for the first time in a long time, she was speechless.

"Holy shit. It's him."

"Ho-ly shit," Ryder muttered under his breath.

It was Mr. Unavailable. Carly's Kryptonite. The one guy who had gotten away, and she'd always wondered 'what if.' He wasn't alone either. He had a very cute, very sweet looking woman with him.

"I need another shot."

"Get me one too," Ryder said.

Carly caught the eye of the bartender who had just waited on Mr. Unavailable and his woman and ordered a round of shots for her and Ryder.

She looked across the bar again. This time, he looked at her, and when those blue eyes hit her, she felt a churning in her gut. The same feeling she'd always had when he looked at her. Uneasiness, mixed with a little self-doubt and a dash of the unknown.

He smiled, and Carly fought the urge to groan. She felt Ryder move closer to her side, standing as Mr. U made his way through the bar to her, new woman in tow.

"Hello, Carly," he said in that gravelly, sexy voice that had always sent shivers up and down her spine.

"Hello, Jack."

"It's good to see you."

"You too," she lied. Ryder snorted, and she resisted the urge to elbow him in the stomach.

"We came down from Lafayette to check on Dad's camp before the storm hits. He's out of town." He motioned to the woman with him. "This is Jessica."

"Hello, Jessica. It's nice to meet you." Carly held out a hand. "Carly Devereaux. My brother and a friend of mine own Snapper's. So glad you guys could stop in."

"Owner, huh?" Jack raised an eyebrow. "I had heard you were in Biloxi."

Carly held back a snort of her own. Biloxi. She had left there over two years ago when she had found her lying sack of dog crap boyfriend in bed with another woman. Ryder cleared his throat—or growled. One or the other, the sound was the same.

Jack looked at Ryder. "Ryder, it's been awhile."

Ryder grabbed a cigarette and lit it before responding.

"Yes, it has." Carly was relieved he didn't say, "Not long enough." Or something equally offensive.

"Play a game of pool sometime tonight?"

Ryder's eyes sparkled. The man was almost impossible to beat at the pool table and would relish giving Jack a good beating.

"Put your quarters up anytime."

Jack nodded then turned again to Carly. "Enjoy your night. It was good to see you."

"You too," she returned automatically. "I need another shot," Carly said as they walked away. "It's going to be a long night."

• • • •

AFTER THE PARTY DIED down, Carly was wiping down the bar and singing along to the music playing on the jukebox. The bar had closed and was empty except for her and Joey.

"You want some help?" Joey asked as he came back in after taking out the trash.

"No, Joey, I'm fine. It's okay. Go home," Carly said as she wiped down the bar. He looked at her, frowning.

"Seriously. I'll be okay. You think some random fisherman is going to come in at two a.m.? Lock the door behind you. I'll be home soon. I promise."

Joey looked like he wanted to argue but he knew better. He was at a standstill. What could he do?

He left, locking the door behind him and leaving Carly all alone.

She popped the top on a beer and put some money in the jukebox. Then she went to stock and get the shift ready for the next day. While she worked, she thought of Mr. Unavailable. How happy he had looked with his new flame. Happier than she'd ever seen him. There was a light in his eyes that she had never seen.

He had never been unavailable. He had simply been unavailable to her.

When the Aaron Lewis song came on about change, she took her beer and went and sat cross-legged on the edge of the pool table. It was then she finally let the tears fall.

"Everything really does change," she whispered as she wiped the tears from her face. "Everything but me."

Chapter Two

. . . .

WHEN CARLY WOKE UP, Joey was gone. His Jeep was still there, which meant he probably ended up riding with Noah in his truck. More room for supplies since they would probably be picking up plywood and other construction equipment.

She grabbed her dogeared and worn journal from the Jack Era from the drawer in her nightstand.

It was no surprise he was on her mind after running into him the night before. She hadn't seen him in years, and she had no idea he would still affect her that way.

Crossing back through the house, she stopped in the kitchen and poured a cup of coffee. She carried the mug and the journal outside and sat on a chair on the deck. Up higher, she could see the waves, and all was clear and calm. The sun sparkled off the water, no lingering signs of yesterday's storm or any upcoming bad weather either. She opened the journal to a page she knew well.

December 1st

Speaking of webs I keep getting stuck in, Jack was the first man I dated after the ex. Seeing the ex's friends apparently sent me into more than one bout of nostalgia. Jack was the first thing I thought of when I woke up this morning, and I instantly reached for the phone. I scrolled through the numbers and breathed a sigh of relief when I remembered I had deleted his number again. As I lay there, I replayed every single memory I had with him. When we met at the Marine Ball I had gone to with Noah.

How handsome he had been in his dress blues. The coffee date, the night out when we went to hear a band play. To the last time I spent time with him at his house over a month and a half ago. I don't know what this urge is to reconnect. The fact that I've gone a week since trying to contact him? I'm sure writing this book doesn't help. Whoever said writing was therapy was full of crap on this one. I have so many regrets with him. Things I didn't say. Things I didn't do. Maybe I still need that closure. Maybe I just can't let go...

With a frustrated sigh, she slammed the journal shut. "I should just throw this whole damn thing off a bridge. How's that for closure?"

With a sigh, she tossed the remainder of her coffee over the deck railing and called for Sammy. She needed some TLC from Glinda at the Redbird. Thank God, that never changed.

• • • •

CARLY PULLED UP IN the driveway of the popular B&B that attracted people from all over Louisiana and the Gulf Coast area. It was especially popular for families and fishermen.

The main house where Glinda lived and served the meals was a classic building on stilts. A deep porch ran along the front of the house, complete with rocking chairs, ceiling fans, and two lazy hounds. Carly had spent many hours in those rocking chairs talking with Glinda and sipping a cup of coffee or something stronger.

The dogs thumped their tails against the wooden floor as Carly and Sammy walked up the stairs. Carly reached down and patted each on the head before entering the house. With so many people in and out during the day, the door was never locked.

The great room of the inn was one of Carly's favorite rooms anywhere. It was a huge open area. A wall of French doors that Glinda opened on pretty days was on one side. Round tables and chaise lounges were on the deck for those who wanted to lie around in the sun.

On another wall was a fireplace and built-in bookshelves filled with books and games. Families staying there could play a game of checkers on the big tables by the French doors. If someone wanted something to read out on the deck, they were welcome to borrow one of Glinda's books. Glinda's own reading preferences were pretty diverse, crime thrillers, non-fiction, and some romance. Previous guests had donated to the collection as well, so there was something there for everyone.

It was still early, so the room was empty. Carly went over and made a cup of strong coffee—Community, of course. Restless, she wandered around the room. She ended up at the display of pictures, one very similar to the one at Snapper's. In fact, several of them were copies of the pictures here. Photos of the Boonies as they'd grown up. Pictures of proms, graduations, gatherings.

"Hey, pretty lady!" Daniel said as he entered. He poured a cup of coffee for himself then said, "Come on into the dining room." They carried their cups into the adjoining room.

"What's new?" Carly asked as she sat at the table, nodding to the newspaper in Daniel's hands.

"This storm in the Gulf. It intensified overnight."

"Is that right?"

"Yes, it's now a tropical storm and shows signs of continuing to strengthen."

Glinda came into the room, carrying a silver serving tray with some of her homemade biscuits and jelly. "Hi, honey! How are you?"

"I'm good, Aunt Glinda." Carly stood to give the other woman a hug then grabbed a biscuit and covered it with Glinda's strawberry preserves. Glinda grew the strawberries herself in a small garden behind the inn. Glinda wasn't actually her aunt, but that was what everyone called her. The only one of the circle friends who could claim her as a real relative was Gabriel, who was her grandson.

"Good, good. It's going to be a smaller spread today. Several of the guests have checked out ahead of the storm, and the cancellations for next week are rolling in. It being the off season, there weren't a lot, anyway."

"Yeah, Joey left this morning to get some supplies. I'll check on the weather this afternoon before I decide to start preparing Snapper's. I have stock I need to put up and other things."

"We're going to head to Austin," Glinda said. "We're leaving in the morning to beat any crowd on the road. You know how it is trying to get out of here if you wait too long. Traffic for hours. This is a great opportunity for us to get away. We can go see Grace and Gabriel. I talked to him this morning, and they are there and not on the road."

"What about the Redbird"

"Noah is going to come by later to help us with anything that needs to be done." Glinda nodded back to the kitchen. "Let me finish up, and I'll come back out and chat."

"You should think about coming to Austin with us," Daniel said. "We were talking yesterday about a trip. This would be a perfect time."

"I would love to, but I better stick around and keep an eye on things. If we close, it would be a great time to try to get some writing done."

Daniel nodded. "True."

"Of course, since I stopped dating, I don't have much to inspire me anymore. I started *All I Want for Christmas,* like, three Christmases ago. Maybe I just need to give it up. Obviously, I'm not going to find him, during the holidays or otherwise."

Daniel muttered something to himself before taking a sip of coffee. "Maybe you need a change of perspective."

"Maybe so. I keep taking it out and reading it, revising, it and submitting, but I'm not having much luck. It's been about as successful as my hunt for Mr. Right."

"You did get a couple of hits from publishers," Daniel said.

"Yeah, but no one's taken it yet. Maybe you're right. Maybe I just need to put it away for a while."

"Whatever works. Maybe it would help if you got together with some other writers and talked about brainstorming and whatnot."

Carly cocked her head to one side. "That's an idea, but where?"

"Oh, I'm sure you could find something. Google it. You can't be the only author around."

She nodded. "I'll do that."

Glinda came in with another tray, this one full of bacon, different kinds of sausages, and eggs. She placed the tray with the others on the sideboard and poured herself a cup of coffee and sat at the table.

"Daniel told you we were heading to Austin?"

"Yes, he did."

"Did he also say you should come with us? Grace and Gabriel would love to see you. And I hear Austin is such a wonderful place for creative people. Maybe you could find some inspiration there. Grace writes music, so maybe you can bounce some ideas around."

"Yeah, we could. That would be great, but I think I'm going to stay here. Keep an eye on things."

"What if you have to leave, Carly?" Glinda asked.

Carly waved her hand. "We haven't had to evacuate in years. Not since I've been back. It's a tropical storm. Just a little wind and rain. Besides, I love the storms. I love to watch them roll in and listen to the rain. That will probably inspire me to write more than anything else."

Glinda exchanged a look with Daniel. "Well, if you change your mind, call me. We're leaving early in the morning. You have plenty of time to get ready."

"I will. You guys enjoy your time. Take a couple of days extra if you want. We'll take care of everything here." Carly grabbed a plate and added a little bit of everything on it. "But I am going to miss your cooking, even just for a few days. Thank God for Joey or I'd be eating sandwiches and canned ravioli."

It was well known that Carly was one of the worst cooks in the parish. When there was any event where food was involved, she was assigned paper plates.

"Take some home, *cher.* There's plenty. And take some for Joey too. Give him some time off."

"I will definitely be doing that."

The rest of the meal consisted of small talk about local politics and upcoming events. Soon, Carly was hugging them and saying her goodbyes.

"Watch the news tonight, and if you change your mind about leaving, let us know."

"I will, but I'm sure I'll be fine. You guys have a safe trip. C'mon, Sammy. Let's go."

As she drove away, a part of her wondered if Glinda and Daniel were right. Was she making a mistake blowing this storm off?

• • • •

"TROPICAL STORM STACIE continues to strengthen as it works its way across the Gulf. Residents of South Louisiana are urged to keep an eye on this storm as it progresses..."

The newscaster's voice continued from the radio in Noah's truck.

"Good thing we brought this instead of the Jeep. I think we may need more than the little bit of supplies we originally thought."

"Yeah, well, you never quite know how these things are going to go. And with the Redbird, Snapper's, and our own properties, we have a lot to take care of. We're going to have quite a haul. And our work cut out for us if it does head this way."

"Ryder sent me a text this morning. He's staying another day in case we need help. He called his boss this morning. They may be packing up and heading north too. Boss said he should just stay where he was for now."

"Good deal. We can use another hand," Noah agreed. "Carly can take care of stock and whatnot at the bar. Do you want her to make a list for your kitchen?"

"She's not touching my kitchen. Either one of them."

Noah laughed. "I can't say I blame you. She'd have no idea where to begin and would still be packing as the place floated away."

"What are we going to do with her?" Joey asked, looking out the window, not wanting to meet Noah's gaze.

"What do you mean?"

"You don't see something's going on?"

"I do, but I also know how she is. You push her, she's going to clam up. She'll tell you nothing's wrong. You talked to Ryder? Sometimes he knows. He'll be around a couple more days."

"Yeah, I'll give it a shot. More than likely he won't tell, though. Remember Grace? He never told us what was up with her. We had to figure it out."

Joey's younger sister, Grace, had come home after living in New Orleans with a secret she had shared with no one.

"I'd still like to get my hands on Brent Mouton," Joey said.

Brent, Grace's former bandmate, had slipped her a roofie and raped her. She'd returned to Bon Chance broken, and it had taken months and Gabriel's friendship and love to help her begin to put the pieces back together.

"Wouldn't we all?" Noah asked. Joey saw Noah's hands whiten on the steering wheel. A run-in with the former soldier and Mouton would not end well for Brent.

"Well, you know why Ryder didn't say anything. How could he? It would have been such a betrayal to tell you, her brother, of all people."

"You're right."

"But ask Ryder about Carly anyway. And if he tells you, let me know. You know, it may be nothing."

"I will." With a frustrated sigh, Joey turned and looked out over the marshland that separated them from the mainland.

Noah, as if sensing the conversation was over, turned up the radio.

Chapter Three

• • • •

JOEY HAMMERED THE LAST set of nails in the plywood covering one of the windows of the Redbird Inn. He stood back and stretched. It had been a while since he'd done construction work. He didn't know how Noah and Ryder did it all day.

Speaking of those two, they had already finished their part of the work and were leaning against Noah's truck. The rocking chairs normally on the porch had been stashed safely away in storage earlier.

"One down, two to go," Noah said, referring to Snapper's, and then Noah's and Joey's homes.

"And the houseboat?" Joey asked.

"Emily and I are taking it out tonight. It will be interesting for a few days. The two of us and three dogs."

"Has anyone talked to Carly? What's she going to do?"

Ryder blew out a puff of smoke and threw his cigarette down, grinding it out in the dirt, "She should have left with Glinda and Daniel this morning."

"What if she has to evacuate? Does she even have a plan?"

"Carly? A plan?" Noah said. "She may have to be prodded on this one."

"Oh, yeah, and who's going to be the one to take that bull by the horns?" Ryder asked.

23

Joey and Noah both looked at him.

"Shit."

．．．．

SNAPPER'S WAS QUIET as Carly walked around, taking mental note of what would need to be done to prepare the bar for the storm. But she had no idea where to begin. In the few years they'd been open, they'd been lucky enough to have only dealt with a tropical storm or two.

Storm surge would be the biggest issue and would take out anything left on the floor. Snapper's was an older building and had withstood many storms before, but it hadn't been raised off the ground as much as some of the newer buildings being built.

Carly spied the wall of framed photos on the back wall. Grabbing an empty box, she went to pack up the memories. In the worst-case scenario, beer could be replaced. These photos couldn't. Some dated back to when "The Boonies," as she called their group, were still in high school.

One day she would scan all the pictures and save them digitally. As she packed them away, she took a moment to remember the time and place each picture represented. Noah and Emily's going away party, before he left for the Marines, and she for college in Lafayette. The last holiday Ben had been with them. The spaghetti cook-off when Emily's then husband, Eddie, showed up and almost ruined the day for them all. And the more recent picture of the barbeque cook-off when the secret Grace had been hiding had been revealed.

She was placing the last picture in the box when the door opened. Turning, she said, "The bar's closed today."

Denis Mouton, a cop in the neighboring town of Pointe Shade, stepped into the building. Carly's pulse spiked, as the man set her nerves on edge. "Stepped into" wasn't so much the term to describe it as much as "swaggered." God's gift to women, or so he thought. The wedding ring he wore did little to deter his transgressions. He flirted with Carly every chance he got. But the worst was when he defended his nephew, Brent, after he had slipped Grace the date rape drug.

"I was just passing by, saw your car here. Thought I'd see if I could offer you any...assistance."

Carly stomach turned over, but she kept her face expressionless. She edged closer to the safety the barrier of the bar would create.

"I'm all good here. I'm sure your...assistance would be better appreciated elsewhere."

"I don't know about that. A pretty little girl like you might need some help. In here, all by yourself." As he talked, he inched toward the empty space the workers used to go back and forth between the bar.

Carly reached down and wrapped her hand around the neck of the vodka bottle in the well. Her other hand felt for the phone in her back pocket.

A few more steps, and Mouton would cross the threshold separating him from Carly.

The door opened again, and Joey, Noah, and Ryder walked in.

"What are you doing here?" Ryder asked.

"Just checking on things around here. There's a storm blowing in, you know," Mouton responded, placing a hand on the billy club on his hip.

"This isn't your jurisdiction, Mouton. You've been told that," Noah said.

"As an officer, it's my duty to make sure I check on ladies left alone."

Carly set the bottle of vodka on the bar with a thud, leaving her hand on it.

"As you can tell, it's all good here. You can go *check* on someone else. And as I said, the bar is *closed*. So, there's nothing else for you here."

He nodded then tipped his hat to the men as he left. "I'd be careful of leaving that one alone too long. You never know who might wander in here."

"God, I hate him! He creeps me out!" Carly fumed as the door shut behind him.

"Carly, this is why I hate leaving you in here by yourself. You know how he is. Look what his cousin did to Grace," Joey said, his attention focused on Carly. "You okay?"

Carly blew out a frustrated breath. "I'm okay. He's gone. Let's finish this up and get out of here."

The men cast one more to look at Carly to be sure she was fine, then nodded and went outside to start working.

Later, Carly pushed the last box onto the top of the bar. With the windows covered, the bar was now almost completely dark. She had turned on the lights, but it did little to fully illuminate the room.

Finished with her work inside, she grabbed a beer from the cooler and leaned against the bar, waiting for the guys to come back in.

She wondered if she should turn on the TV for an update on the weather when the alarm rang from her phone.

She pulled it out and saw it was an emergency alert. The tropical storm warning was now a hurricane warning.

Light flashed as the guys came in and flipped on the local news.

"There is now a voluntary evacuation called for the citizens of Jefferson, St. Andrews, and St. Raphael parishes." As Bon Chance was in the latter parish, the people of the town were being encouraged to leave.

Noah picked up his phone and dialed. "Emily?" he asked, "could you come to Snapper's?"

Only a couple of blocks away, Emily arrived soon after his call.

Carly protested. "Come on, guys. Do you think it's really going to be that bad? It's only a one at this point. People have stayed for those. We'll barbeque, be without power a few days, maybe. It will be fine."

Noah replied, "Carly. We need to get out of here before they tell us we have to. Then it's mass chaos. We have to get past New Orleans, and possibly Baton Rouge, and it's going to be bumper to bumper if we wait too long."

"But where am I going to go?" Carly asked. "And I have Sammy."

"Carly, we're not leaving here without you," Joey said. "*I'm* not leaving here without you."

"I hate to be the asshole, but while we sit here and argue, we could be getting other things done and ready to go," Ryder said. "I'm going to go back to Houston. That's far enough out of the way, by what the map says now, and I need to get back to work."

"I can go with you, then," Carly said to Ryder.

His eyes softened as he looked at her. "Carly, I live in a camper. It's perfect for me, but it's not the place for both of us. And a dog."

Emily said, "I think I have a plan. Remember my friend, Gemma? She owns the sandwich shop by the Cypress Café. She sent me a text earlier. She'd seen the weather. She's living with Jasper now, and her old apartment is empty. She said any of us could use it if we needed a place to go. Why don't Carly and I go to Lafayette? It makes more sense for me to go there so I can be close to the cafe. And I can bring my van and get it in a safer place. If something happened, insurance would pay for it, but I need it for upcoming jobs. I'd rather not have to have it repaired or, God forbid, replaced right now. These things can take forever."

For a moment, Noah looked as if he would disagree, not wanting to leave Emily, but apparently seeing the logic, he nodded. "Joey? You coming with me?"

Joey looked at Carly as if torn. Finally, he said, "Yes."

"It's settled, then," Ryder said. "Let's get everything secured and boarded up and hit the road first thing in the morning."

Chapter Four

TUESDAY, SEPTEMBER 30th
  One Day Before Landfall

• • • •

THE RAIN BEAT DOWN on the tin roof as Carly shut the lid to her suitcase with a sigh.

"That's it, Sammy. You ready?"

The old dachshund tapped her tail on the floor in response. Sammy was always up for a ride. Carly wondered what the dog would think of this new adventure. If there were treats and naps involved, she would be good.

With Carly's stomach in knots, she was envious of the dog's laidback attitude.

This would be okay. They would be gone for a couple of days, then be back, and everything would be back to normal. They were just being safe.

She rolled her suitcase out into the living room. Joey sat at the bar and looked at her as she came in. He chewed on his bottom lip as if he wanted to say something. He twirled the mug of coffee in front of him in his palms.

"Joey," Carly started, wanting to say so many things. *I'll miss you. What am I going to do with you not around? Do we really have to do this? Do I have to leave?*

"Yes?" he asked.

Terrified, she only replied, "Will you fix me a cup? Emily will be here soon, and I want to make sure I haven't forgotten anything."

A shadow fell across his face. "Of course."

Idiot, she chided herself.

"Thank you," she said as he handed her a mug of coffee. A nod was his only response. Maybe a few days apart would help put the mess that had become their relationship into perspective.

"You ready?" Noah asked, reaching out for her suitcase as Joey carried out the last box.

"Yes," Carly said, "as I'll ever be, I guess." After a last look around, she followed them out the door.

The rain beat down as Noah ran out to the van. After giving Emily a longer than normal goodbye kiss, he escaped back into the safety of the porch, leaving Joey and Carly alone in the rain.

"I guess I'll see you soon," Joey said.

"Yeah, I guess," she replied.

He reached out and pushed a strand of wet hair out of her face. "Carly?" His quiet voice was almost drowned out by the falling rain.

"Yeah?"

He leaned down and kissed her softly on the lips. A surge of electricity jolted through her body unlike anything she'd ever felt.

"Be careful, okay?"

Speechless, she only nodded.

"Now, go on and get out of this rain. Text me when you get to Lafayette. Noah and I are leaving right behind you."

"Yes," she whispered.

Joey shut the door, giving her a small wave as she put her vehicle in gear and followed Emily out of the driveway.

• • • •

JOEY WATCHED AS SHE drove away, ignoring the warm rain as it beat down on him, soaking his clothes. Carly was leaving. It would be the first time in a couple of years that they wouldn't be within literal shouting distance. They hadn't been apart since she'd moved back from Biloxi after she left A.J.

He knew she hadn't been happy in a while. She seemed kind of stuck in neutral. Not going forward, and not going backward. Carly, being Carly, always put on a happy face, even when she wasn't feeling it. He'd been worried about her; she'd been drinking way too much. Another sign of her general displeasure with life. Where it came from, he wasn't sure. He didn't know if she knew why she was so unhappy. This time away could be a good thing for her, even just for a couple of days. But for him?

He walked into the house, and already it was too quiet. It was like Carly took the very essence of the home with her. He walked through the house, his footsteps loud in the silence. After changing into dry clothes, he poured himself another cup of coffee and sipped it, leaning against the counter.

Noah came back in, as if he'd been giving Joey a moment or two alone. "You about ready to go, man? That weather is turning nasty quick. The water will be rough."

"Yeah." He poured the coffee into his travel mug and placed the cup in the sink beside Carly's discarded one. "We better get going."

• • • •

CARLY WAS STILL THINKING about Joey and that kiss as she pulled up beside Emily's van in the small driveway of the garage apartment. Sammy jumped out and immediately began inspecting her surroundings as Carly got out and stretched. It had been a long drive, mostly slow going due to the intermittent rain bands they'd had to go through. They had apparently beaten the bad weather for now. The sun was out in Lafayette.

A petite woman with flaming red hair stood from one of the rocking chairs on the second story porch.

"Hi, Emily!"

Emily smiled and waved. "Hey, Gemma! We were going to come meet you at the shop for the key."

"Well, since you texted me at four a.m. and it's now one in the afternoon, I figured you'd been in that car about long enough," she said as she came down the stairs. "I walked from the shop."

Carly noticed the woman's "Bite Me" t-shirt and grinned.

"You must be Carly. I'm Gemma." Gemma bent down to welcome the women's dogs. Emily had brought along her Boston terrier mix, Oscar, a big black and white dog with a round head and goofy, pointed ears.

"It's nice to meet you. And thank you for letting us stay here. Hopefully, the weathermen are exaggerating as they do sometimes."

"Well, it's better to be safe than sorry."

"Yes," Emily agreed. "And the evacuation became mandatory a few hours after we left. We were lucky to get on the road when we did. It was still a tangled-up mess of traffic."

"Do you need some help? I can call Jasper if you need."

"Honestly, I'd love to sit and eat and relax for a moment."

"Why don't you come by the shop? Lunch will be my treat," Gemma said. "And feel free to bring your dogs along. We have an outdoor seating area they will love."

"That, my friend, sounds like a plan. Lead the way."

Carly walked behind the two women, at a slower pace to keep up with Sammy's little legs. There was a steady breeze blowing, and the clouds from the storm were slowly rolling in.

She took in the sights as they made the short walk to Gemma's sandwich shop. Carly loved the city already, with its small parks, artwork on every corner, and the street musicians playing here and there. It was like New Orleans, in a way, but smaller. And cleaner.

They reached Bite Me and were soon placing their orders. Gemma waited outside with the dogs while they ordered.

When they returned, Carly and Emily sank down into the chairs. Carly slung her feet up into the empty seat across from her. She took a long sip of her beer and blew a wayward strand of blonde hair out of her face.

"This place is awesome," Carly said, casting a glance around the courtyard area. Several round tables dotted the outside eating area. Big, green leafy plants were nestled in the corners.

"Thank you," Gemma said. "It's been a long process, but we've come a long way."

An employee came out with their orders and a request for Gemma. "Excuse me," she said, getting up. "Let me know if you need anything. When you get ready to go back to the apartment, let me know."

"Will do," Emily said. "Have you sent Joey a text yet?" she asked Carly. "Or Ryder?"

"I was about to. I was waiting to get halfway settled." Carly grabbed her phone and typed in the messages to let the two know they had arrived safely. As she put the phone back down, she wondered what Joey's response would be.

"Those clouds don't look very promising," Emily said, looking up to the sky.

"I know," Carly agreed. "We may have left Bon Chance only to get hit by the storm here in Lafayette."

"At least it won't be as bad. No storm surge. I wonder how the guys are faring on the boat."

"I'm sure they're fine. They have plenty of food and beer to keep them busy. We may need to make some kind of run when we finish here. As bad as I hate to get back in the car after that drive."

"When we get back to the apartment, I'll see what we need. I may be able to grab some things from the café."

Carly took a bite of the Philly steak sandwich in front of her. "Man, this is good!"

"Aren't they awesome? Noah and I usually stop in when we're here. And we like to stop in and see Gemma, and Julien if he's here, but I don't see him today. He might be busy with this storm coming in. He works in construction with his two brothers." Emily grinned before continuing. "Those are three fine specimens of men if I've ever seen them."

Carly smiled. "Is that right?"

"Oh, yeah. They did the work on the café. And talented too. Lucky is quite the photographer. If you go look in the restaurant, Gemma has put some of his prints on display."

"Wow. I'll have to go back in and look." Carly picked up her beer, holding it up to note that it was empty. "It looks like now is a good time to go see. You ready for another one?"

Emily looked at her own bottle. "Yeah, I could use one more. Especially after that drive."

Carly grabbed the two empty bottles and tossed them into the trash as she walked back into the building. Before she walked up to the counter, though, she looked around the room until she spotted the prints on the wall.

These are gorgeous. Swamp scenes with cypress trees dripping with Spanish moss, a lone boat on the water surrounded by the purple hues of sunset, and old, gray abandoned church covered in ivy in the shadows of massive oaks.

"Amazing, aren't they?"

Carly turned to see Gemma behind her. "Yes, very."

"I'd say you should meet him someday, but he can be quite the character. He's the cousin to a friend of yours, Ryder, I think?"

"Oh, Lord," Carly said, laughing. "I don't think they make them ornerier than Ryder."

"You may just have to see for yourself."

"If I'm here that long. I'll need to get back to Bon Chance."

"I understand that," Gemma said. "Running your own business can be quite time consuming."

"Yes, it can. But it might be nice to have no responsibilities for a day or two. Speaking of which, I came in here for a couple more beers. I better get them before Emily wonders where I ran off to."

"Enjoy. I'd join you for one myself if I could. Maybe later."

"Of course," Carly said, "I'm always up for a cold beer."

Gemma laughed. "You and me are going to get along just fine. Come on, let's get you that beer, then I'll go with you and Emily to get ya'll settled in the apartment. Weatherman just issued a tornado watch."

· · · ·

AFTER THEY FINISHED eating, the trio walked back to the apartment. Gemma chatted throughout the trip, talking about downtown and some of the changes and how well Art Walk was doing now that it had cooled off.

"Emily, have you thought of opening the café for that night? Noah's furniture would be a hit."

"I have. But the weekends are my busiest with the catering. It's hard to justify pulling manpower away for one night. Maybe something to consider in the future, though. Especially with the holidays coming up."

"Definitely. I've been adding a bit of stock myself. I'm expecting the next couple of months to be very busy."

"That's good. I'll give it some thought. Maybe I can do some juggling with the girls' schedules." As they approached the apartment, Gemma said, "When I grabbed my hurricane supplies this morning, I grabbed some extras for you as well. I got a couple flashlights, some water and ice, extra oil for the hurricane lamps. There's a small grocery store at the intersection where the light is, but I'm not sure what they'll have at this point. I'm sure you know how it is when a storm rolls in. It's like the end of the world."

"Thank you so much," Emily said.

"You're very welcome. Can I help you unload?"

"I think we got it," Emily replied. "We don't have too much."

"Okay, then, I'll get back to the shop. I have a few things to attend to there."

Gemma hugged them both. "Text if you need anything. And keep me posted on how things are here."

"Will do," Emily said before turning to Carly. "Let's get this stuff unloaded, then I'll head over to the café and check on things. You still want to make that grocery store run?"

"You got it," Carly said. She looked up at the sky. "We better get a move on. It looks like the big rain will be here soon."

The storm clouds twisted in the darkening sky. The wind picked up too, whipping through the trees and smelling of rain. Carly felt a churning in her own stomach, a sense that something bad was coming. Had they made a mistake coming to Lafayette?

• • • •

CARLY FOLLOWED THE directions Gemma had given her and soon was pulling into the crowded parking lot of Albertsons. It was so full, she had to take a spot close to the busy street, Johnston, she had just turned off of. A little walk wouldn't hurt. She needed to work off some nervous energy, anyway.

She grabbed a stray cart on the way, not knowing if they would have any when she got in there, and surveyed her list again. It was pretty simple, the basic hurricane supplies, plus stuff for gumbo. It was an unwritten rule that when a storm came, gumbo was made. It may be chicken and sausage, shrimp and okra, or seafood in general, but when a storm was brewing, you made a gumbo. It was a good thing Emily knew how to make one, because Carly had no idea where to even begin.

She was glad she had grabbed the cart when she walked into the store because there were none up front and the store was full of people. As she turned the first corner, it was chock-a-block, like a grocery store rush hour. Everyone wanted the same things at the same time.

I need a drink. She sighed and longed for the laidback attitude of Bon Chance. She had a feeling that today there would be no "how ya doin?" or "how is your mom and dem?"

She pushed through the aisles picking up gumbo ingredients, bell peppers, celery, onions, and roux. Then the paper goods and water. She almost bumped a cart or two on the bottled water aisle that was almost empty. It was as if the zombie apocalypse had begun.

Her phone dinged as she waited for a grocery store employee to pull out another pallet of bottled water. *I hope they're paying him overtime.* People began pulling off shrink wrapped bundles before he stopped.

She grabbed her phone to see that Joey had messaged her.

Joey: Wyd?

Carly: Grocery shopping.

She grinned as she waited for his response.

Joey: Emily trusted you with that?

Carly: Boo, I can follow a list. I just can't cook what's on it.

She resisted the urge to laugh out loud in the aisle. Seeing that there was some water left, she grabbed a package and put it in the cart. She sighed. Was this storm really going to be that bad?

Rain poured down as Carly pushed the cart full of groceries out to the parking lot. The walk was long, and her hair was soaked. The puddles on the ground seeped through her shoes. The wind whipped again, chilling her wet body.

She wiped her face dry only to have more water drip down from her hair. "I wish I was anywhere but here."

Chapter Five

SAFELY ANCHORED IN a harbor just outside of Lake Charles, Joey and Noah took a moment to relax. Noah leaned against the counter of the galley kitchen with a beer in hand as Joey cooked, his body and drink rocking with the rhythm of the boat. Aaron Lewis's latest album played softly from speakers in the corners of the room.

"How do you think the girls are doing?" Joey asked as he diced onions on the small cutting board. They had bought all the ingredients for gumbo when they had made a supply run before setting out. Finished with the onions, he dumped them into the Magnalite and went to work on some plump green bell peppers.

"I don't know. I heard from Emily a couple of hours ago. She said the wind was picking up as the rain bands came in."

Joey nodded. Carly had told him the same thing. "I didn't think it was going to get that bad in Lafayette."

"You never know with these things. They should still be fine. They are far enough inland."

"True."

"What's going on with you and my sister, by the way? You're all stuck in your head tonight."

"I kissed her," Joey blurted.

"You kiss her all the time."

"No, I mean really kissed her. In the rain. Before she left." Joey still had the memory of her lips pressed against his seared his brain. *Damn storm.* If she hadn't needed to go, he would have pulled her in his arms and...

"And?" Noah prodded, smiling.

"She didn't say anything."

"Carly didn't talk?"

"No."

"You left my sister speechless?"

"Apparently so."

Noah raised his bottle in salute. "Cheers to you, my friend. It's about damn time."

Joey smiled and raised his own bottle and tapped it with Noah's.

"So, now what?"

"I have no idea," Joey admitted. "Not a clue."

"You're kidding me, right? All this time, and you have no clue what you want to do? Why don't you just ask her out?"

"Like, on a date?"

"Yes, like a date. Where you take her to dinner and all that?" Noah laughed. "You know what you should do? Take her to New Orleans. Go out to a nice place to eat, listen to some music after. She would love that."

"You're right. She would." Carly loved New Orleans, and Joey enjoyed going with her. She embraced the city's atmosphere, and it was like she became a living, breathing part of its rhythm.

Noah nodded to the phone that lay beside Joey's cutting board. "Why don't you ask?"

Joey frowned. "I will. But not now. Not in the middle of a hurricane, and not over the phone. I'll ask when she gets back to Bon Chance."

Noah said, "Sounds like procrastination to me. But I'm going to hold you to that."

"You do that." Joey laughed. "Now, isn't there a football game on or something? Or would you like to discuss your relationship with Emily now?"

"Touché." Noah reached for the television remote, signaling the end of that conversation.

· · · ·

"I NEED TO LEARN HOW to cook," Carly said as she leaned against the kitchen counter watching Emily cut up the sausage for the gumbo.

"It's not that hard," Emily said. "You can help me if you want."

"Emily, I have a hard time boiling water. It's best that I give you moral support."

"I think you could do it if you really wanted to."

That old self-doubt crept in. "I don't know about that." She swiped her phone to switch the song playing.

"One of these days, come over and I'll teach you. We'll start simple. Like Grandma Ruby started with me." Emily smiled as she grabbed a wooden spoon to stir the sausage she had just put in the black cast iron pot. "This is her old pot, by the way. I brought it along."

"Grandma Ruby. I miss her."

"I do too, so much. I think she would be happy with us now. With me and Noah together. She always did try to push us together whenever possible."

"She was a wise woman."

"Then he went off to the Marines, and I came here for school. We just grew apart. Then I married Eddie..." Her voice trailed off.

"It all worked out in the end," Carly said.

"Yes, it did."

The wind whipped up again and drove rain against the window. Carly paced to the door and looked out. It was dark outside. All she could see was the shadows of tree limbs bending to the force of nature in the streetlights.

Their phones buzzed with the newest weather alert, and Carly jumped. "I'm so tired of these alerts."

"What is it this time?" Emily asked, cutting potatoes for what would become potato salad.

"Flood warning. Like we would be going anywhere in this weather, anyway."

"We're good. We're up high. Gemma said she'd never had any flooding here. Not even last year when the whole area flooded. And we still have power."

"True."

After they finished eating and cleaning up the kitchen, Carly peeked out the window, looking at the steady stream of rain. It blanketed the area in front of the apartment, a shroud of impending destruction. The wind roared as the rain beat against the windows. The sound was constant, like the snowy sound on a TV when the channel went offline.

The storm had picked up speed as it traveled the I-49 corridor and worsened more than predicted.

As the wind howled, she continued to watch the shaking street sign and chunks of trees falling into the street. "We really left Bon Chance for this?" Carly asked.

Emily glanced at her phone, looking for the latest weather report. "Apparently so."

"You want another drink?" Carly asked as she finished off her beer.

"Um, yes. What else do we have to do?"

Carly grabbed two longnecks out of the fridge and returned to the living room. She sank down on the floor in front of the coffee table.

"You think the guys are faring better than we are?" Emily asked. "Maybe they should have come here with us."

Carly thought of Joey, and her stomach flip-flopped. "They should be okay. You haven't heard from Noah?"

Emily frowned. "Not yet. It could be a cell phone tower issue. You haven't heard from Joey?"

Carly sighed. "No."

"What's going on between you two, anyway?" Emily asked.

The wind whistled around the apartment finding its way into every nook and cranny of the older building. Sammy nestled in close to Carly on the couch, finding refuge under a throw blanket.

"I don't know," Carly said. "It's gotten so complicated."

"What's complicated about it? You guys are friends, aren't you?"

"Yes, we've always been friends. Something's just different now."

Emily smiled. "I wonder why."

"What do you mean?"

Emily shook her head. "If you don't know by now, girl, you're either blind or clueless."

What Emily implied sent tremors of fear through her body, almost like the jolt she'd felt when Joey had kissed her. "Joey?"

"Joey."

"No. That can't be. We're just friends. Anything else would mess that up."

"You never know. Why don't you ask him out?"

"On a date?"

"Yes." Emily rolled her eyes. "A real date. Where the guy buys dinner and everything. How long has it been since you went on one of those?"

Carly sighed. "Good Lord, too long."

"Carly, what do you have to lose? Joey isn't going anywhere. Go and enjoy a night out away from Bon Chance and Snapper's and see what happens."

Carly looked down at her phone. Emily had a point. "Maybe so. He is my Mr. Right."

"Your Mr. Right?"

"In my phone. He's been Mr. Right in my phone forever. It's a joke that started years ago." Carly went and grabbed her journal, flipped through a few pages before handing it to Emily. "Read this."

I do have a Mr. Right in my life. His real name is Joey, and he is another one of my best friends. We grew up together too. Ryder is a few years younger than I am, while Joey and I are the same age. How did Joey get this nickname? A few weeks ago, we were hanging out together, and he and I were having a big discussion about where my life was going. Did I really want to bartend forever? What did I want to do? Bar work has a shelf life, and no one really wants to be slinging drinks when they're fifty. In the midst of this mid-midlife crisis I seem to be having, I talked with Joey. He gave me some advice, and like always, it was dead on. I needed to figure out what it was that made me happy and go for it. Later that night, I sent him a text message.

Are you right all the time?

My phone rang. It was Joey, and I answered, "Hello."

"Yes, I'm always right," he said. He hung up without saying anything else. No hi, no bye, nothing. I giggled a little and texted him again.

Does that make you my Mr. Right?

He did not respond. He doesn't think it's as funny as I do, apparently. Because of this, he's still in my phone as Mr. Right. He's not happy about it. He frequently mentions that I am not to tell anyone he's my Mr. Right. Why? I don't know. I think it's pretty funny.

"Well, honey, I don't know about signs and all that, but don't you think that might be one?"

"I'll text him tomorrow."

"I think you definitely should."

"What should I say?"

"Um, how about 'Joey, let's go out'?"

"We go out all the time. That's all I need, for him to think it's a regular night out while I'm thinking it's a date."

"Say 'Let's go out on a date,'" Emily suggested.

"I'm too old for this," Carly said. "I feel like I'm back in grade school. I'll think of something. You think we need to check that app again? How long is it going to take for this thing to blow over, anyway? And how do you think Bon Chance is faring?"

"I guess we'll just have to see," Emily said. A tree limb scraped against the window, making them jump. Emily and Carly both gave their dogs reassuring pats on the head.

"For now, all we can do is wait it out."

Both women jumped again as a boom resounded and the apartment was plunged into darkness.

"Shit."

Chapter Six

CARLY AWOKE TO THE sound of someone walking around in the courtyard. She and Emily had opened the windows when the storm had lessened enough to allow a breeze in so they could sleep.

She glanced over at Emily, who was still asleep on the couch. Another crunch on the yard spurred her into action. She grabbed a can of wasp spray out of her bag and tiptoed out of the apartment.

"Sammy, stay here. I'll be right back," she whispered. Oscar cocked one big ear in her direction, and she hushed him.

Taking one step at a time, she slowly made her way down the staircase. A man walked around the mess of fallen branches and leaves, cursing in Cajun French.

She held up the wasp spray. "I'm armed, and I'm not afraid to shoot."

"What are you going to shoot me with, *cher*?"

Carly held the black bottle out in front of her. "This."

"Boo, I'm here because Gemma asked me to come. You can shoot me with that if you want, but if you do, you'll have to answer to her, and she's a lot meaner than I am."

He grinned, and Carly put the can down. "I'm sorry. I didn't realize. I'm Carly," she said, putting her hand out.

"Lucien. But most call me Lucky."

"Lucky? The picture guy?"

He raised a golden eyebrow. "Picture guy?"

"In the sandwich shop. You have photos there."

He smiled, flashing dimples that would scramble any woman's ovaries. "Yes, that's me. Gemma is nice enough to let me put them in there, and I do sell one or two every now and then."

Carly stared at him. He really was one of the finest specimens of men she'd seen in a while. His eyes were bright blue and sparkled with mischief, his sun streaked blond hair a little long and unruly. He was tanned and rugged. One could tell he worked with his hands. She resisted the urge to wonder what else he was good at with those hands. It was way too early for that.

"I'd offer you coffee," Carly said, "but our power's still out."

"Well, I guess it's good I came prepared. I have a thermos in the truck. You have a cup?"

"I'm sure we do. I'll go get it. Would you like to come up?"

"Sure."

He went to his truck as Carly headed in to grab a couple of mugs. Emily was just waking up when she came back in.

"Lucky is here. He's working on the tree that fell in the yard."

"Lucky's here? Give me a minute, and I'll come out. I haven't seen him since he and his brothers finished up the café."

"I'll tell him you're coming. I'll grab you a mug too. He brought coffee."

Emily smiled. "Ohmygod, he's an angel."

"Have you seen the man? Angel is not the word I would use to describe him."

"He's hot, huh?" Emily said.

There was the sound of a throat clearing on the porch, and both ladies exchanged sheepish glances realizing the object of their conversation had heard them through the open windows.

"Damn storm," Carly said.

"I'll blame it on the lack of coffee and sleep. My brain is not functioning correctly."

"Yeah, mine either, apparently," Carly said. "I'm about to take care of that, though, and get me some coffee at least. Kinda glad the power's out, and I didn't have to make the coffee this morning. I am not the best brewer in the world."

"Go, girl, get you some coffee. I'll be out there in a minute. I need to walk Oscar too."

Carly took the two mugs and went out the screen door. "Emily will be out in a minute. I think you know her?"

"Oh, yeah, we did the reno on her café. Good people," he said. "Here, give me that cup. You look like you could use some caffeine."

"Gee, thanks," Carly muttered.

"Or it was the conversation I overheard," he said, grinning.

"You are kin to Ryder, aren't you? I see it."

"Shoo. I taught that boy everything he knows."

"I bet that took a whole minute or two."

Lucky threw back his head and laughed. "No one gets too much over on you, do they?"

"I had to learn. Your cousin would dance circles around me if I didn't."

Lucky finished pouring the coffee and handed her the mug, "I'm not one for cream, sugar, or any frou-frou. If you want that, there may be some in the apartment."

"It's okay, I'm sure," Carly said. She grimaced at the first sip. "Man, you like your coffee strong!"

He laughed. "Only way to drink it."

"Yeah, I think I'm going to go see if we have anything to thin this out. After one cup of this, I might be able to move that tree myself."

Emily came out as Carly was going in. She greeted Lucky with a hug. "It's so good to see you again. How are things at your place?"

"Not too bad, a few limbs down. Jasper is working on clearing the limb damage around his house. He wasn't sure he could make it here, so he called me. Power's out at our house, of course, but we have a generator. Gotta keep the beer cold," he said with that grin.

"A man after my own heart," Carly said. "But, sadly, ours is getting hot."

"Which is why I'm heading to the café to see how things are there. I'll bring back some ice from the machine, if we have any," Emily said as she joined them on the porch, ice chest in tow.

"Need some help?" Lucky asked.

"Only for you to tell me what you'd like to eat. I'll need to cook up some of our meat before it spoils, and I have to throw it away."

"Whatever you want to cook. I never turn down a home-cooked meal."

"Good deal. I hope Gemma has some charcoal around here. I was thinking of barbequing."

"If not, we can find some, I'm sure."

"Cool. Let me go take care of this. Do you need anything?" Emily asked them both.

"No, ma'am," Lucky said as Carly shook her head in response. As Emily walked away, Lucky said, "Well, before it gets much hotter, I should probably finish with that tree."

"Do you need any help?"

"Actually, if you'd haul the smaller stuff to the curb while I cut, that would help tremendously."

"I can do that."

"Great. I'll owe ya."

Carly followed him down the stairs. Lucky went to his truck and retrieved a set of gloves that he gave to Carly. The leather was soft, well worn, and way too large for Carly's small hands. Still, the protection they provided from the rough wood was welcome.

"Well, *cher*, let's get to work," Lucky said as he picked up the chainsaw he had left by the tree.

Carly took a deep breath. It had been a long time since she'd done any kind of labor like this. Usually, the guys took care of all this. How long had it been since she'd actually had to do something on her own?

Too damn long. Maybe it was time. The chainsaw growled in the quiet neighborhood as Lucky sliced through the first branch.

Carly grabbed the branch. It was heavier than she expected, and she stopped. For a moment, she wondered what she had gotten herself into. Could she do this?

She pulled on the limb again, this time digging in with her legs. It moved easier that time, and Carly was able to turn and pull the branch to the curb.

Dropping it, she turned around, beaming. Lucky was smiling back.

"I was going to get that one. But you go, Super Woman," he said as she returned.

Super Woman. I could get used to that.

• • • •

TIRED, MUSCLES ACHING, Carly flopped down on the chair on the porch. Lucky handed her a beer from the ice chest he had toted from the bed of his truck.

She held the cold bottle up to her flushed cheeks. "What I wouldn't give for some air conditioning right now."

"Right?" Lucky agreed. "But just sip on that and enjoy the breeze. You'll cool off before you know it."

"You could be in here," Emily said, her voice drifting through the open kitchen door. "It's hotter than Hades."

"Come out here," Lucky said. "Grab a cold one and take a break."

"I'm almost finished with this, putting the last bit of seasoning on the steaks. If you could light up the pit, though, that would be great. I found some charcoal in the storage room. I just need to remember to get another bag to replace it."

"I can do that." Lucky grabbed another beer before he disappeared down the steps.

The screen door opened, and Emily stepped out. She took a seat next to Carly.

"I talked to Noah. Their cell service finally returned. They're fine. They've already left for Bon Chance to check everything out. It shouldn't take them long. It will be faster by boat than by road, I'm sure."

Bon Chance. Snapper's. Taking care of the tree had kept her mind off the hurricane, at least for a moment. With no electricity, there was no news, only what the women had seen on social media before they'd turned their phones off to save the batteries. She would just have to wait to see how the town had fared. Patience was not one of her virtues.

Lucky returned. "Pit is lit. I moved it from the courtyard over to the side of the house. Easier to keep an eye on. No breeze in the courtyard either. The high fence keeps it out." He leaned against the railing of the porch. "Any word from home?"

Emily related to him what she had just shared with Carly.

"If y'all want, you can use my truck to charge your phones. I didn't think of that earlier, or they could have already been charging."

"That's an awesome idea. Thank you so much. I feel so cut off from everything," Emily said. "Want me to grab yours when I take mine down there? You're looking a little worn out."

"Thank you for showing up today. You've been a godsend," Carly said to Lucky as Emily went to put the phones on charge.

"When Jasper told me you two were here alone, I knew I needed to come check on you. We LeBlanc men are a little old fashioned, I guess."

"Well, we do appreciate it."

"I get fed and get to spend time with two fine looking women. It's a win-win."

Carly rolled her eyes. "Next thing, you're going to ask if I want to get naked and throw potato salad."

Lucky laughed. "Ryder's still using that old line? I guess if it works for him. I have my own lines, and trust me, they work."

"Emily? You need some help? The stuff is getting deep out here!"

"I hear him. Remember who his cousin is."

Lucky held hands up to his heart. "How you wound me!"

"Yeah, yeah," Carly said. "Why don't you find us some music to listen to or something? It's too quiet with just the sound of the birds."

"I can do that, *cher*."

Lucky clomped down the metal stairs and back to his truck. He turned on the radio and opened the driver's side door. Cajun music began drifting on the lightly blowing wind, along with the scent of charcoal from the now blazing pit.

"Hello!" Carly looked down to see a neighbor waving from his back door.

She waved back. "Hi!"

"Sounds like a party."

"It is. Want to come over? We have plenty."

"Would love to. Thank you."

The man appeared to be in his early fifties. Tall, gray-haired, and a killer smile. When he appeared on the porch, Carly was taken in by his smile and electric blue eyes.

"Name's Gibson," he said, extending his hand. "You must be Gemma's friends."

"Yes," Carly said. "We came here to weather the storm, but we didn't escape much, apparently."

"I hear the coast got hit pretty bad. The storm surge wasn't bad, it was the wind."

Carly's heart dropped. Snapper's had been there forever, though. Surely, it had made it through this storm too.

"I'm Carly," she said. "This is Lucky. Emily is finishing up a few things in the kitchen."

"Hey!" Emily called, hearing her name and the introduction. "I'll be out in just a moment. But I know you already. You come into the Cypress."

"I make my rounds."

Emily came outside, wiping her hands on a towel. "Gibson is a regular. He takes a walk through downtown every day. He stops in at the Cypress, Gemma's shop, and then Legend's."

"Best happy hour in town," he said.

"Best one, huh?" Carly said. She'd have to check that out.

"Oh, yeah," Lucky agreed. "Beer's cold, service is excellent. Burgers are good."

"Sounds like an awesome place."

"I'll be right back. I need to check the fire," Emily said.

"Why don't we move down there?" Lucky asked. "We can bring the chairs. There will be more room and possibly be a bit cooler."

Everyone grabbed a chair and carted them to the area around the barbeque pit. As everyone joked, talked, and listened to the music from Lucky's truck, Carly realized how wonderful this idea had been. How long had it been since she just let herself live in the moment?

It had been way too damn long since she'd been this relaxed. Way too damn long.

Chapter Seven

JOEY AND NOAH WERE quiet as they drove down the highway toward Bon Chance. They had docked just outside of Houma, where Joey had left his Jeep on higher ground. Downed trees littered the sides of the road, billboards advertising charter trips were bent or broken, and the overall damage left Joey with rising anxiety.

Rounding the corner into town, Joey couldn't believe what he saw. Some camps had been completely destroyed and were nothing more than piles of lumber. The damage was sporadic, though, as some buildings looked completely undamaged.

"Everything could be okay," he said, thinking of their homes, Snapper's, and the Redbird.

"Where do you want to go first?" Noah asked.

"We can go by your house."

Pulling up to Noah and Emily's, Joey felt relieved. Other than some missing shingles, the house appeared to be fine. A quick walkthrough confirmed the house was unharmed.

A short drive later, they were at Joey's. A downed power line kept them from venturing too close, but from where there were, everything seemed okay. The next stop was Snapper's.

There, Joey's heart sank as he looked at the destruction. Brightly colored curtains flapped through broken windows. Carly had picked those out herself. The Snapper's sign had broken in half and swung like a pendulum in the wind. One side of the building was completely gone. He could see the sun glistening off the silver beer coolers. The inside was totaled, the wind and rain destroying everything.

"Wind damage," Noah said, his voice raspy. "Must have been a small tornado."

Unable to speak, Joey nodded.

The surrounding buildings had received minimal damage. Some missing shingles, a broken window here and there. Easy fixes. Those were newer, though, and although they had upgraded Snapper's when they remodeled, it was still an older structure.

Joey walked toward the boat dock behind the bar, carefully dodging boards and other debris. There was nothing left. It was simply a few posts poking out of the water.

He thought of growing up, of him and Carly sneaking bottles of alcohol and cheap cigarettes. Carly with her feet dangling in the water and talking about the future and adventures.

"What are we going to tell Carly?" he asked Noah. His voice was hoarse and barely above a whisper.

"We have to tell her the truth. Snapper's is gone."

Joey could only nod.

"We'll go check on the Redbird for Glinda, and then we'll hit the road to Lafayette. No use putting it off. If the power gets restored there, she may see it on the news before we can tell her."

"She's going to be devastated."

"I know. But she has us."

Joey felt a sinking feeling in his gut. This was not going to be good.

• • • •

"STOP! STOP! YOU'RE killing me!" Lucky gasped, flexing his booted foot.

"I told you I can't dance." Carly laughed.

"I didn't believe you. I thought everyone in Louisiana could dance."

"Nope. Not me. I've always wanted to but just can't."

She had tried to tell Lucky that she really couldn't dance. Ryder had tried to teach her, to no avail.

"I've never met a woman who couldn't dance."

"You have now."

"I can't believe Ryder has been holding out on me." Lucky winked at her. Carly merely rolled her eyes.

"Whatever."

Lucky's blue eyes darkened for a moment before he pulled down his sunglasses.

Carly looked down at her beer and peeled at the label. Needing an escape, she said, "Excuse me," and headed into the house for a bathroom break.

Once there, she took a few moments to gather her thoughts. Lucky made her nervous. Something she hadn't felt around a man in a long time.

She exhaled a deep breath before heading outside. A complication with a man was not what she needed. Besides, in a few more days she'd be back in Bon Chance, slinging beer at Snapper's. She stopped to fluff her ponytail. Maybe a little harmless flirtation was just what she needed to take her mind off things back home.

Coming down the stairs, she noted the conversation stopped when she was spotted. Obviously, they had been talking about her, because Emily looked down at the ground and not at Carly. Probably telling Lucky to keep his distance, Carly thought. Whatever she said had obviously worked, because he looked at her with a touch of sadness in his eyes.

"Well, I think I need to hit the road," he said.

"Me too," Gibson agreed. "It's been a long day."

Carly was disappointed that the party seemed to be over. Everyone said their goodbyes, and the guys took to-go plates and headed to their homes.

Carly had just plopped down into her chair when Noah's truck pulled up. Ryder's truck was right behind them.

"You didn't tell me Noah was coming. Or Ryder..." Carly looked at Emily, who glanced away. Unease prickled through Carly. Something was wrong.

Joey stepped out of the truck, and he and Noah walked up to her. Looking in Joey's eyes and seeing the sadness, her heart dropped.

"What is it?"

Joey reached out for her hand and rubbed it softly for a moment before raising his eyes to hers.

"It's Snapper's, Carly. It's gone."

"What do you mean, gone?"

"The storm. It must have been a small tornado. It..."

Unable to hear any more, Carly turned and walked away.

• • • •

JOEY EXPECTED A LOT of responses, but complete silence was not one of them. Carly simply clammed up. She grabbed another beer out of the ice chest and walked off to the enclosed courtyard and closed the gate.

"Should I go after her?" Joey asked.

"I wouldn't. Not now." Ryder lit a cigarette and opened the ice chest and grabbed bottles for everyone.

"It's going to take some time to sink in. She's put so much of herself into that bar to make it work," Noah said. "And then we'll have to decide what to do next."

"She's going to want to rebuild." Joey took a sip from his bottle and sank down into one of the lawn chairs.

"We may have to decide what's logical, though. You saw that building, Joey. There's not much left. And with the new building codes after Katrina, will it even be worth it? It will take twice as much money." Noah sounded as if he was already doing the figures in his head.

"She needs to get out of the bar business, anyway," Ryder said. "She's not going anywhere. She's unhappy. We all know that. Yeah, she tries to put on a happy face, but we know better. And you? What about you, Joey? What do you want to do? It's your bar too."

"I don't want to go back to the oilfield. That's not for me." He tried not to shudder thinking of the fourteen-day shifts.

"And if we don't re-open Snapper's?" Noah asked.

He exhaled. "If we don't reopen Snapper's, I'd like to go to culinary school in New Orleans. I've been thinking about it for a while, actually."

"That's a really cool idea," Emily said. "You could do so many things with that."

Noah nodded. "That is cool. And I would have more time to work on my furniture."

Ryder said, "I think it's kind of settled. We'll give Carly a few days to process this, then we can talk to her."

. . . .

CARLY SIPPED HER BEER and listened as the rest of them talked. They were deciding her future, and she wasn't even getting a vote. What would she do without Snapper's? Fear gnawed at her stomach and made her pulse pound. Noah had his furniture, and it seemed Joey wanted to go off to school in New Orleans. What did she have? A big nothing. No job, nothing. Bon Chance wasn't exactly brimming with employment opportunities either. She would probably have to leave town to find something that paid anything. More change.

Carly wanted another drink, but she didn't want to face the others. They had no idea she had overheard them, and Carly didn't want to clue them in.

She twirled the empty bottle in her hand, watching the sun sparkle on the glass. Empty, she thought. Just like me.

. . . .

JOEY WATCHED THE GATE, waiting for Carly to come back out. It wasn't like her to go off by herself for long. She didn't like being alone that much. He grabbed a bottle out of the ice chest and made his way to the courtyard.

She didn't acknowledge him when he came through the gate. She simply sat there staring at the empty bottle in her hand.

"Hey, Carly. I brought you another beer," he said.

"Great. Thanks." Her voice was flat.

He walked around so he could see her. She wouldn't raise her eyes to look at him. He reached out with the bottle, and she took it. He sat in the chair opposite her.

"It's going to be okay. You know it?"

She snorted. "Is that right?"

"It is. Everything can be replaced."

She laughed. "Oh, really? And rebuilt?"

Joey felt a little shiver of unease at her tone. He looked down, unable to look her in the eye. How could he tell her there would be no rebuilding?

"Joey?" Her voice was hoarse, barely over a whisper. "How long was it going to be before you told me?"

She knows. His blood went cold. She had heard them.

"Carly..."

"Don't Carly me. I heard it all."

He reached out for her hand, and she snatched it back.

"No," she said. "You don't understand. I poured my life into that place for the last two years, and now you want to walk away from it."

"It's not that, Carly."

"Then what is it? Because New Orleans sure sounds a lot like walking away. You're walking away from Snapper's." Her voice caught. "And you're walking away from me."

"Carly, I would never walk away from you."

"But you are. You all are"

"Carly..."

She stood and walked across the small courtyard. "Just go, Joey. Just go."

His heart breaking, he turned and walked away.

• • • •

CARLY BRUSHED AWAY a tear as she heard the gate swing shut. She didn't have to turn to know who it was. It could only be one person.

"I don't want to hear it, Ryder."

"Well, that's just tough, and you know it. You're going to hear it anyway. I don't know what you said to Joey, but judging by his hangdog expression when he came out of here, it wasn't good."

"What do you care?"

"Really, Carly? We're going to play this game? What are you so mad about?"

"I heard you all talking. You aren't rebuilding Snapper's. And you aren't even asking me what I think."

"Ooooh," he drew the word out, "so that's what this is about. Well, why don't you come on out and tell us how you feel? Nothing is set in stone. Hell, everything just happened. We all need time to think about this."

"We? There's no 'we.' If it weren't for you, they wouldn't have had this conversation. Some friend you are."

He was silent for a moment, and Carly knew she'd gone too far, but her hurt and anger kept her from taking the words back—not like she could, anyway.

"Ben was my friend, and I miss him too, but I also know he'd want me to have a happy life. Not be chained to the shrine I'd created in his memory."

"You think that's what this is?"

"That's exactly what this about. You've done nothing with your life since his death. Yes, you opened a business, but it's eating you alive. Why do you think I wanted you to come see me in Houston? I wanted you to get out. You need a change, Carly. We all see it, but haven't said anything, and that's our fault. Use this as a chance to start over. Write. Go back to school. Do something. Be happy."

She turned around, tears still falling down her cheeks. "What if I don't want to start over?"

"Well, then, you're just being an idiot. This is sudden, but that's how life is sometimes. Carly, we all love you. You know that. Take a few days, enjoy some time off, and think about what you want to do."

He held out his arms, and Carly stepped into his embrace. She inhaled, relishing his familiar scent of leather, cigarette smoke, and cologne.

"What are you so afraid of?" he asked, his voice raspy.

"I'm not afraid of anything." She sniffed.

He laughed. "We're all afraid of something."

"Oh, yeah, and what are you afraid of?" As far as she knew, Ryder, who for fun rode bulls that could kill him, was not afraid of anything.

"There's one thing I'm afraid of, but we can talk about that later. Let's get you situated, and one day we'll sit and talk."

"I'm going to hold you to that."

"I'm sure you will."

"Will you ask Joey to come back?"

He cocked his head to one said and gave her the Ryder grin, complete with dimples. "I will."

He enveloped her in his arms again and kissed the top of her head. "I love you."

She sniffed as she wiped away a tear. "I love you too. Always."

He reached for her hand and squeezed it before he walked away.

· · · ·

THE GATE OPENED AGAIN, and Carly looked down at the ground before meeting Joey's eyes.

"I'm sorry," she said before raising her head.

"It's okay, Carly. It's a lot to take in. And I'm sorry we talked about it without you. That wasn't fair."

Carly looked up into his brown eyes. "It's okay. Maybe Ryder is right. Maybe this is all for the best." She thought of sitting on the pool table a few nights before and crying. Deep down, she knew they were right. It was time for a change.

"What are you going to do?" he asked.

"I don't know. I guess we will see. It's been a long time since I really sat and thought about what I wanted. I think it's time."

"What can I do?"

"Go enroll in culinary school. And send me recipes and pictures from New Orleans."

His eyes widened. "Recipes?"

"Hey, a girl has to feed herself."

He laughed. "I'll believe that one when I see it."

She punched him in the arm. "Oh, ye of little faith."

"I've always had faith in you." He reached out and brushed his hand across her jaw, and Carly's legs went weak. Yesterday, she had been determined to ask him out and act on everything she'd been feeling. Today, everything had changed.

She reached up and placed her hand on his. "Joey?"

"Yes?"

She leaned in and pressed her lips to his. He responded by wrapping his arms around her and pulling her close. His kiss was more urgent than the last one. As if he knew it would be the last one for a while.

Carly had never felt like this before. His kiss, his touch felt so right. But how could it be when everything else in her life was so wrong?

She took a step away from him and smiled.

"Let's go out and talk to the others," she said. Decisions needed to be made. He hugged her and held her close for a moment, then they went out to talk to the group.

• • • •

JOEY SAT ON ONE SIDE of her and Ryder on the other. It was the protective stance they always took with her. However, they couldn't protect her from the aftermath of Mother Nature's fury. Joey grabbed her hand and held it reassuringly. She smiled when he squeezed gently.

"Snapper's is a total loss?" she asked, needing the affirmation again. It was still so hard to wrap her head around.

Noah nodded. "And rebuilding will take money. We would have to rebuild to the new codes post-Katrina. It would have to be completely redone from the foundation up. Sure, insurance will take care of some, but is this what you want to do? Do you really want to be saddled with all that again?"

Carly looked down, not sure of what she wanted to do.

Emily said, "It's okay if you want to think about it. We don't want to pressure you at all. Here's something I think you should consider. I need someone to take care of the café. I'd like to expand, and running it and the catering company is spreading me too thin. Right now, we're only open for lunch, which means we are missing out on the events that happen after that, like Art Walk and Well Alive, that could bring in more business. With your experience, this could be such a great opportunity."

"I could do that," Carly said. "But what about a place to live?"

"You could live here. Gemma has already asked me if I'd like to stay here during the week, so I didn't have to commute. I'm sure she would be happy to work out something for you."

Could she do it? Could she leave Snapper's? Bon Chance? It didn't seem like she had much choice at the moment.

She looked at Joey, who smiled at her reassuringly. Joey who was about to start on his own adventure. She said, "I think it sounds like a plan. For now."

Emily smiled. "That is awesome. I'm so glad you said yes! I have so many ideas."

Noah looked over at his girlfriend. "Why don't we give her some time to get adjusted? Then we can inundate her with plans."

Emily laughed. "Of course. We can come back sometime next week when things are all settled and talk."

Come back. That meant they were leaving. Carly would be alone. In a town where she barely knew anyone. Terror crept through her veins.

"I'll stay with you for a few days if you want," Joey said. "I can't get back to my house anyway because of the power lines."

Carly was tempted but was terrified of what would happen if he did. She was already distraught over losing Snapper's. It would be so easy to lose herself in the comfort of his arms, but she knew it was the exact thing she didn't need to do. That would only lead to disaster.

"I don't think that's a good idea," she said. It was her turn to squeeze his hand. "I think this is something I need to do on my own."

"Is there anything we can do for you before we leave?" Noah asked.

"Turn on some electricity?"

"That I cannot do." He laughed. "But with the hospital not far away, it shouldn't be long before it comes back on. That will be their first priority."

"It seems like everything is settled. Carly, you know I'm always here for you, but I need to get back to Houston to work," Ryder said. "Maybe now you'll come see me."

When he stood, Carly did too. He said his goodbyes with hugs and handshakes, and she walked him to his truck.

"You're going to be okay," he said, giving her one last hug. "All this is going to be okay. You'll see."

"I hope you're right."

Carly held on to him for a moment, not wanting to let get go of the security he provided. Security that was quickly blowing away.

He hugged her close before backing away. He winked. "I'm always right."

She slapped his arm. "Go on. Asshole."

He gave her one more grin, and she watched as he drove away.

"Hey, Carly? We're going to head out too," Noah said. "Joey is going to stay in the houseboat until he can get to his house."

Carly walked over to her brother and gave him a hug. Emily had gone up to collect her suitcase.

"Call me when you get home."

"Will do."

Emily came down with her suitcase. Noah opened her van door so she could load it. The van door slid shut, and Noah gave her a last hug. As Emily backed out of the driveway, Carly was struck by the scene that was so similar to a couple of days before. Only this time, Carly would not be returning to Bon Chance.

Noah climbed into his truck, leaving her and Joey alone. She could see him in the truck scrolling through his phone to give them as much privacy as possible.

"This is not how I thought today would go," Joey said, stepping closer to her. He reached out and smoothed her hair behind her ear.

"Tell me about it," she replied. "I have no idea what to do now."

"I know one thing," he said, leaning down to kiss her. Carly felt the tingle that was becoming a familiar feeling as his lips touched hers. She sighed and leaned into his embrace, wrapping her arms around his waist. He deepened the kiss, and the tingle turned into a hum that vibrated through her body.

She could ask him to stay, and he would. Loyal Joey. Always there for her. They could wake up naked in the morning. But then what?

Placing a hand on his cheek, she stepped back.

"The house isn't going to be the same without you," he said. "I'm going to miss you."

"I'm going to miss you too."

"I'll see you soon?"

"You will. I'll come this weekend and grab some things. Maybe. I don't know. I don't know if I can stand to see Snapper's yet." She felt her bottom lip quiver and looked away.

Joey touched her chin with a curved finger. "You don't have to if you don't want to. If you let me know what you need. I can bring it."

The thought of Joey packing her clothes, her panties, was more than she could take. She laughed. "I'll let Emily know."

"Gotcha." He leaned down and kissed her softly one more time. "One day, Carly, we're going to settle this. That's a promise."

"Once and for all, huh?"

"Once and for all."

After one last hug, he turned and joined Noah in the truck.

She watched as the truck turned the corner, leaving her alone. Completely alone. She couldn't remember the last time she'd been on her own. She'd lived with the ex-boyfriend in Houston, the ex-fiancé in Biloxi, and now she lived with Joey. She had taken up residence in one of Glinda's cabins for a bit, but that wasn't like living alone. There was no one at the big house to come save her if something went wrong here. No one to cook for her, no one to have coffee with, nothing.

With a sigh, Carly walked up the stairs to the apartment. She put out her hand to open the screen door but hesitated. Inside would be too quiet. And in there she would have to face the fact that in the span of twenty-four hours her life had done a one-eighty. Instead of going in, she grabbed a beer from the ice chest. She popped it open and took a seat on one of the rocking chairs on the porch. She leaned her head back, resting it on the back of the wooden chair, and sobbed.

Chapter Eight

CARLY GROANED AND CLICKED "yes" as the message on Netflix asked for the umpteenth time, "Are you still watching NCIS?"

"I don't know why you keep asking me that," she said to no one. "It's not like I haven't been lying here like a slug for the last day."

The power had come back on shortly after everyone had left, and for that Carly was extremely grateful. It was easier to wallow in self-pity when there was air conditioning and Netflix.

She'd seen every episode of the show, and some more than once, but somehow the familiarity was a comfort to her. Something that was still the same in her life.

She clicked "continue" and was greeted by sights and sounds of New Orleans instead of the usual Washington D.C. area.

"Great…Just great."

The bridge over the Mississippi loomed large for a moment, lit up for the night. Then the popular restaurant, Muriel's, stood proudly on the corner. The red building had been on Carly's bucket list forever. She wanted to dine at the haunted table and have a drink on the balcony, preferably around Halloween.

Halloween was in three weeks. She should be planning a party for Snapper's, decorating. Contemplating her own costume.

A tear dripped down her cheek. Joey had sent her pictures of the destroyed Snapper's earlier, and it had been her undoing. Seeing all she had worked for in ruins had brought her to her knees. She was sorry she had asked him to send the images. She hadn't responded to him, unable to form the words to reply.

She'd been in bed since, lain there for so long her body had begun to hurt almost as much as her heart did.

On the TV, a scene from Café du Monde had her wishing for beignets and *cafe au' lait*. The sweetness of the powdered sugar of the doughnuts, the sun, and the energy of the French Quarter would be a comfort right about now.

Her stomach growled, and she looked at the time on her phone, once again ignoring the texts from Joey, Ryder, and her brother.

"Thank God for delivery."

If she were in Bon Chance, Joey would cook something for her, if only to make her feel better. Or Glinda would whip up one of her favorites. But she wasn't in Bon Chance anymore. And there was no one to take care of Carly, except for herself.

"Sammy," she said to the dog snoozing at her feet, "I don't think we're in Bon Chance anymore."

. . . .

IN BON CHANCE, JOEY glanced at his phone.

"That's like the fourth time you've looked over there. Why don't you just call her?" Noah asked.

They were in Noah's outdoor kitchen, preferring the cool breeze over the stuffiness of the house where power had not yet been restored. The sound of the generator that kept their refrigerator going hummed loudly in the background, almost drowning out the music playing from the radio.

"I don't know. I sent her a goodnight text and a good morning text, and she hasn't responded to either of them. She hasn't responded to Ryder either. I asked him."

Noah flipped burgers on the grill. "She's okay. Emily talked with her earlier today to make plans to meet to talk about the café."

Joey breathed a sigh of relief. She had been upset. She had tried not to show it, but that was Carly. Always trying to put on the happy face. "What do you think she's going to do?"

"I have no idea," Noah said, shrugging. "Probably run off somewhere."

Joey's heart sank a little. It was true. Carly had a history of running when things got too tough. It was one of the major reasons he'd been afraid to make a move on her. She'd run from Houston and Biloxi to return to Bon Chance. But this time, where would she go?

He exhaled a deep breath and looked at his phone again.

How could he convince her to stay?

• • • •

CARLY OPENED THE FRIDGE door and peered at the contents inside. A few leftovers from yesterday's barbeque, some beer, and the few staples they had grabbed when they came into town before the storm was all that was there.

Carly considered warming up the leftovers. She wrinkled her nose. The food had been good the first time. She wasn't sure she wanted to eat it a third time.

How did one get to be her age and not know how to cook something? It was a basic life skill to be able to boil water or fry an egg. Yet Carly had never seemed to master either. There was always someone else to do the dirty work, and she had gone with the flow.

Tomorrow, she would go to the store and buy eggs. Maybe YouTube would be able to teach her how to scramble an egg. Until then, she would have to rely on other sources, and Carly was damn tired of relying on others.

She leaned against the counter. She shook her head, disappointed in herself for not seeing how dependent she'd become. She thought of herself years ago, when she'd packed up and moved to Houston, taking the hotel job. She'd been so excited for the new opportunity. She was going to conquer the world. Now she couldn't master a sauce pot.

She snorted. "Some independent woman I am."

She opened the fridge again, as if expecting something new to have magically appeared in the moments since she opened it last. Seeing the bare shelves again, she resisted the urge to slam the door. Instead, she grabbed her phone. "Takeout it is. I wonder if they'll deliver from the Redbird?"

Sammy tapped her tail on the floor in response. "I know, girl. I want to be there too. I could use some of Glinda's *pain perdu*, French toast. Or better yet, some of Joey's homemade spaghetti and meatballs." But no one was cooking much there either, since the power still had not been restored. Now they would all be gathered around the barbecue pit, cooking, playing some music, and having a good laugh or two. Without her.

Loneliness hit her like a punch in the gut. She looked at the phone in her hand. One call, and she could go back.

Jazz music played from the TV again, making her think again of New Orleans.

She could move to New Orleans with Joey. With her degree and experience, she could get a job bartending at a cool spot in the Quarter. She could walk the streets and daydream and create stories about the people she passed.

Joey could go to school like he wanted. Life would be grand. He wouldn't say no. He'd made his intentions well known when he left.

"One day, Carly, we're going to settle this. That's a promise."

She shivered again, thinking of that kiss. How could they live together again when everything was so different? You couldn't kiss like that and still pretend to be just friends. Kisses like that went somewhere, and right now Carly was not in a place to go down that path. That was the one thing guaranteed to lead to disaster.

"This is all so messed up. My life is a mess."

Ryder was in Houston, and he was safe. There would be no awkward transitions from friends to lovers. She could get a job at the hotel again. She'd left there on good terms. She'd have stability, benefits, could get her own place, learn to cook, maybe even write.

But there would be no Joey. He would be six hours away. Not the three hours he was now. He'd be even closer when he moved to New Orleans.

She looked around the small kitchen. She did have her own place here. And she'd told Emily she would help with the café. She did kind of know a few people here now. Gemma from Bite Me, the nice guy next door, the hot guy with the killer smile.

She grinned. That guy had danger written all over him. She'd do best to keep her distance. Luckily for her, there would be no reason to spend much time in Lucky's presence.

The talk on the TV turned to po' boys, and Carly's stomach growled again. She was in definite need of sustenance. Comfort food, preferably. She fired up her phone again and began scrolling through her choices.

None of it was cooked by Glinda or Joey, but it would have to do. For now.

Chapter Nine

THREE DAYS LATER, BANGING on the wooden door woke Carly from her fitful sleep. Sammy growled her displeasure from under the blankets as Carly flipped them back to see who was causing such a commotion.

She pulled the door open a crack to see Lucky on the porch. Coffee thermos in hand.

Opening the door, she frowned. "What do you want?"

"Well, aren't you a little ray of sunshine this morning." He looked her up and down. "You look like hell. No wonder Ryder called me."

"Ryder can kiss my ass." Carly grabbed the thermos and headed into the kitchen to pour a glass.

"Choo, girl, look at all these takeout dishes. Don't you ever cook?" He nodded toward the white Styrofoam containers poking out of the top of the trashcan.

Carly glowered at him as she added some cream and stirred the coffee. "Why are you here, again?"

"Ryder called me. He's stuck in Houston, and he's not liking the responses he's getting from you. He sent me over here. I can see why."

"Call Ryder and tell him I'm just fine."

"You see, Carly, Ryder's my cousin, and I haven't lied to him before, and I'm not going to start now. Don't believe me? Go take a look at yourself in the mirror."

Carly frowned and took a sip of coffee. She did need a trip to the bathroom after being so rudely interrupted. "Do me a favor and take Sammy outside."

"Will do."

Carly carried the mug with her to the bathroom, needing the pick-me-up the jolt of caffeine would bring.

She placed the mug on the counter and looked in the mirror. Her eyes widened as she saw her reflection. Her red eyes were swollen and puffy, dark circles lining the undersides. The shadows were only magnified by the paleness of her face. Her blonde hair was matted and all over the place. She had done nothing but cry, drink, and watch TV for the last four days.

Lucky was right. She looked like hell.

It was time to make a change. Or at least take a shower.

She turned the water on to the hottest temperature she could take and started scrubbing away days of grief. She deep conditioned her hair and washed with her favorite scent, an orange and mint mix called Happiness.

Twenty minutes later, she was joining Lucky and Sammy on the front porch. Sammy had taken up residence in his lap. The traitor.

"Better?" she asked.

"Much." He took a sip from his cup and leaned back in the rocking chair, his long legs stretched out and rested on the porch's railing.

"You know what?" he drawled. "I've got all day off. Why don't you and your dog load up with me and get away for the day?"

"Where we going?"

"Do you have to ask so many questions? What else you got to do today?"

Carly crossed her arms over her chest. "I have lots to do."

He raised a golden eyebrow. "Oh, yeah? Like what?"

She tried desperately to think of something, anything, but came up with nada.

"See? Come on, I got big plans for us today."

• • • •

ABOUT THIRTY MINUTES later, they were pulling up in front of an old bait shop and bar that reminded Carly so much of Snapper's her heart constricted. Lucky bounded out of the truck, as did his basset hound, Duke. The old dog had done nothing but sleep the entire drive. Sammy had taken up residence in Carly's lap to look out the window, eager to see what adventure awaited. Carly had to admit, she was curious as well.

"This is your big plan? What is this?"

"Follow me."

Carly followed him down the fishing pier to where a boat was anchored. Lucky climbed in and reached out for Sammy, who willingly jumped into his arms. She immediately began walking around the boat and sniffing. He held out a hand for Carly.

"Your chariot awaits."

"This is some chariot." She laughed as she took his steadying hand and joined him in the boat.

"C'mon, Duke!" he said, and the dog showed a surprising amount of agility and bounded in. He took a spot in the front, his big nose in the wind.

"It's been forever since I went fishing," Carly said as Lucky pulled the boat key out of his pocket and started up the engine.

"It's about time, then. Let's get going. We have dinner to catch."

"Dinner? You're that confident we'll catch enough to eat?"

"Ah, *cher*, I wouldn't be out here if I wasn't. Would you grab us a beer, and I'll get us going?"

Carly retrieved two bottles from the ice chest and took a seat. Both the wind from the water and the sun did wonders on her psyche. But, the water always had a soothing effect on her. She wondered if Ryder had shared that tidbit with his cousin.

As she looked at Lucky, his hat on backward, skin tanned from the sun, she knew this was not something he had just decided to do. He lived to be outdoors. It was just the way he seemed to fit out here.

He would make an interesting character in a novel, she thought and immediately wished she had brought her journal. Ryder was right about one thing; she needed to get back to writing. Pulling down her sunglasses, she let her mind wander.

• • • •

LUCKY CAST HIS REEL out and looked over at Carly, who had fallen asleep in the sun. Her dog Sammy, and his dog, Duke, stretched out beside her, also enjoying a little afternoon nap.

Asleep, her face was soft, all traces of grief gone. Who wouldn't be sad, though? The business she'd built herself was gone. Ryder had given him a bit of a heads up in the phone conversation they'd had that morning.

He cast a glance on the bobber floating on the water, then on Carly.

She was a beautiful woman. That soft, dirty blonde hair, those blue eyes, and that flash of spirit. She didn't wear too much make-up or put on airs. She was just the kind of woman he was looking for. He wanted to put the moves on her himself. He didn't understand why Ryder hadn't.

"Go and check on Carly, will you?" Ryder had asked him that morning.

"Okay, why?" Lucky responded.

"There's something going on with her. I just know it."

"Is this one of your fillies?"

"No, and she's not going to be one of yours either. One of my best friends has feelings for her, and she has feelings for him. They're just too pigheaded to admit it."

Lucky had smiled. "I gotchu. I'm off today. The hurricane. I'll drive over there and see how your girl is doing and call you back."

Thinking of that conversation, Lucky grabbed his cell phone and snapped a quick picture of Carly sleeping so peacefully on the bow of the boat. He sent it to Ryder.

It wasn't long before he got a response.

Ryder: Perfect. Thank you, my brother.

Lucky: Anytime. But next time you send me a beautiful woman, could you make sure she's available?

Ryder: LMAO. Like I'd send you beautiful, available women. I keep those for myself.

Lucky rolled his eyes and tossed his phone back in his tackle box. He sang along with the music on the radio and turned his attention back to fishing.

• • • •

CARLY WOKE TO THE SUN beating down on her face. The boat had stopped its rhythmic rocking and picked up speed. She rubbed her eyes and sat up. Sammy was still at her feet, but Duke had taken up residence in the pilot's seat, while Lucky drove the boat, the dog's big ears flapping in the wind.

"You awake?" Lucky called over the sound of the waves slapping the sides of the metal boat.

She nodded, sliding her sunglasses back down to protect her eyes from the sun and the wind. It was like being on a motorcycle, with water. She took in all the wonder of the sun setting on the swamp. The yellows and pinks reflected off the water, the cypress trees casting their shadows. Gorgeous now, Carly was not so sure she'd want to be out when the sun went down, and all the creepy crawlies came out. The gators, the snakes, and God knew what else.

Lucky was quiet as he steered the boat to the dock. Conversation would have been hard anyway over the noise of the radio, wind, and boat engine.

Soon they were pulling into the ramp. Lucky maneuvered the boat close and helped Carly and the dogs off. He tethered the boat and tossed her a twenty. "That bar over there is Turtles. Go in and buy us each a beer. There's a spot outside the dogs can stay. I'll be there in a few."

"You don't need help?" Carly asked.

"Boo, I've been doing this before I could legally drive. You don't know many coonasses do you?" He smiled. "I got this, *cher*. Go enjoy yourself. Duke, go along with the pretty lady."

The basset hound sat on the pier.

"Go on."

Duke turned his head and lazily scratched one of his big ears.

Lucky sighed. "Okay, you and Sammy go on. Duke and I will follow."

Carly stuffed the twenty in her pocket. "C'mon, Sammy."

Sammy took one disdainful look at the hound, raised her nose, then trotted along behind Carly.

Carly walked around the weathered gray building to the deck area in the back. "Sammy, sit."

Sammy jumped into one of the chairs, and Carly went to the window to place their order. The bartender promptly returned with two ice cold bottles. Carly took them to ledge that overlooked the boat loading area. She watched as Lucky expertly loaded the boat onto the trailer and pulled it out of the water.

He parked the truck and walked over to where Carly and the dogs were waiting. Carly handed him his beer.

"Thank you, ma'am."

"Thank you."

"Won't you come in? Meet a few people?" he asked.

"What about the dogs?"

"Does this look like a place that snubs their noses at dogs?' Carly smiled. "No, it doesn't."

She followed him into the bar, where the sounds of Lynyrd Skynyrd played from the jukebox. The buxom bartender greeted him with a smile, and he kissed her on the cheek. Carly could definitely see his resemblance to Ryder.

He introduced her to the few regulars seated around the bar. It was a small place, much smaller than Snapper's, but cozy.

He slapped a few people on the back, shook some hands, and talked some fishing. As they finished their drinks, he asked, "You ready?"

Ready for what? Instead of speaking, she merely nodded. The day had gone so well, why not roll with it? What else did she have to do? Another night of Netflix?

After a few goodbyes, they were loaded back in the truck and headed out.

"I caught enough fish today to fry up a few. I figured after seeing all those takeout trays, you could use a little home-cooked meal."

They didn't talk much on the short trip, just listened to the radio. Lucky sang along to some of the songs, impressing Carly when he was able to sing them in French. Soon they were pulling up in front of a small Acadian style home. Lucky jumped out of the truck, as did Duke, leaving Carly and Sammy to follow. Lucky grabbed the fish and headed off to an area close to the brown water of the bayou.

"You can come watch me clean them if you want. But some are a little squeamish. If you'd like, you can go ahead into the cabin and make yourself comfortable. He tossed her a key. "Sit out on the back deck if you want. But don't let your dog wander too far. We don't have many gators around, but you never know when one will take a swim by."

Carly's eyes went wide. "Come on, Sammy."

Lucky laughed. "You are a city girl, aren't you?"

Carly had never really considered herself a city girl before, as Bon Chance was barely a community, but compared to this, her hometown was a metropolis. She walked up the wooden stairs that led to the raised cabin, loving the porch swing and dog bed.

Out on the deck, Carly sat in the Adirondack chair, feet up on a wooden table, watching the world drift by on the bayou.

Well, maybe not the world, but a few stray logs and a boat or two. She kept one eye out for alligators, but so far had not seen any. Sammy perched on the edge of the deck, watching for trespassers and intruders.

She'd found the sound system and had some eighties rock playing. She sang along to some of her favorites, feeling more like herself than she had since the storm. She should text Joey and Ryder, who had both sent messages, but she just couldn't. Not yet. She needed some time to process this. Decide what to do. Could she rebuild Snapper's and hire a new cook so Joey could still go to New Orleans? And Noah, who had been the resident handyman since they opened, would she be able to find a new person to handle all that? It wasn't fair to them to ask them to stay on if they had other things they wanted to do. That would mean running the bar and restaurant completely on her own. She hadn't the slightest idea how to run a kitchen. And Emily wanted her to run the café?

The back door swung open, and Lucky came out on the deck. He held the door open for Duke, who meandered through.

Lucky sat on the seat next to Carly. "It's a great view, isn't it?"

"It is. It's so quiet here."

"One of the best things about it. We grew up in a house kind of like this one. Jasper lives there now. I live in town in an apartment with Julien, but we built this a couple of years ago. You can take the Cajun out of the swamp, but not the swamp out of the Cajun. We got the best of both worlds."

"Julien is your brother?"

"Twin."

"There's two of you?"

He grinned. "Yes."

"Good Lord."

"I'm the better looking one, though."

Carly shook her head. "I'll just have to see for myself."

"We'll all have to go out together one night. You still need to learn how to dance."

"I'm hopeless."

"Nonsense. That's all in your head. We started with a hard song. I'll start off slow, I promise."

He winked, and Carly looked away. The way his voice had deepened slightly was doing things to her nervous system.

He laughed and stood. He went over to the burner and propane tank and began setting up to fry the fish. He retrieved a big gray pot from the cabin and filled it with oil.

"I'll be back out in a bit. You want to just sit out here and relax?"

"Sure." He'd already seen what a disaster she was at dancing. She had no desire to show him her dismal kitchen skills.

He went back in, and, restless, Carly walked to the edge of the deck and leaned against it, resting her arms on the railing. The sun was just setting, casting the sky and the water in a deep purple. The cypress trees were black silhouettes in the background. The night animals were beginning to come out, the bullfrogs and cicadas, and others Carly didn't want to think about. Carly took a deep breath and exhaled. There was a lot she didn't want to think about right now.

• • • •

LUCKY CAME BACK OUT onto the deck with the rest of the materials he would need in hand. He looked at Carly, silhouetted in the setting sun, her blonde hair floating softly about her shoulders, and something in his gut did flipflops. If she were any other woman, he'd set down the things in his hands, walk over to her, pull that luscious hair to one side, and lay soft kisses on that area just under her ear.

His body tightened at the thought. This was not good. Needing a distraction, he busied himself with cooking. He hummed along with the eighties song playing as he dredged the fish in the eggs and cornmeal before putting it in the hot oil. In another fryer, he dropped small round hushpuppies he'd thrown together. He made it a point to concentrate on the food and not the blonde beauty. If he followed his train of thought, he may burn dinner and skip straight to dessert.

He muttered a curse under his breath, damning his cousin to nine levels of Hell as he threw more fish in the fryer.

· · · ·

"IT'S READY!" LUCKY'S declaration chased away the cloud of thoughts in Carly's mind. Food was a good thing. Simple. Necessary. And after days of takeout, a homecooked meal was a treat.

She took a seat at the table that held a veritable feast of fish, hushpuppies, and coleslaw. "You did all this?"

"Well, yeah, *cher*. We don't get Waitr out here." He laughed. "I like cooking. It relaxes me."

Carly didn't think he was the type to get stressed out, with that dimpled smile and laidback attitude, but she knew as well as anyone how easy it was hide behind a façade. Hadn't she been doing that for months, pretending to be happy-go-lucky bartender, all the while wanting something more?

"Miss Carly," Lucky interrupted her thoughts, "tell me something about yourself."

She was speechless for a moment. Everyone she was normally around knew everything about her.

He laughed before saying, "It's not a trick question, *cher*. And this isn't a date. No need to impress. It's just me."

She took a drink of her own before blurting, "I want to write."

"Why don't you?"

"I'm busy. The bar takes...took a lot of my time. Then it was like the words just wouldn't flow."

"I hate to state the obvious, but it looks like you have more time on your hands now. Don't see what's standing in your way."

"But," she protested, not able to find a reasonable argument.

"But what?"

He was right. She had no argument. She had the extra time now. If she wanted to write, now was the time.

"You're right, you know." She held out her bottle to toast. "No more excuses."

"No more excuses." He grinned impishly. "Now, if you find yourself needing some inspiration for some sexy scenes, I'm your man."

She threw a napkin at him, careful to avoid the citronella candles that dotted the tabletop. "Stop."

He winked. "Baby, I haven't even started."

Wide-eyed, Carly gulped, not wanting to think of things he could start.

Laughing, he said, "Relax, Carly. We're just having fun. I think you need a little after the last few days."

"You are right about that too. And thank you."

"The pleasure is all mine. Now, let's finish this food before it gets all cold."

"Now, that is a great idea." Grabbing a couple more pieces of fish, Carly dug in. Just for tonight, she would enjoy good food and company. Tomorrow was another day.

Chapter Ten

CARLY WRINKLED HER nose as she took a sip of the coffee she'd brewed. Maybe she needed one of those fancy one cup machines. Surely, she couldn't mess that up. She added some more half and half, hoping that would help. It did, but not much. Frowning, she took the cup and her journal and headed out to the porch. If she was going to start writing again, she might as well start now.

She put the coffee on the small side table and opened the book, pen in hand. She took a deep breath and put the pen to the paper. And nothing came.

Thirty minutes later, she slammed the journal shut in frustration. She raised the cup to her lips and grimaced when it was cold. If she had thought it was bad when it was hot, it was even worse cold.

She stood and tossed the remains over the balcony. She might as well start all over. This time, she would use less grounds. The previous cup had been so strong, she might be wired for the rest of the day.

She went back in the kitchen and discarded the rest of the pot and started a new one. As it started percolating, Carly went back outside to enjoy the beautiful day. Having worked nights, she hadn't been an early riser. It was amazing how much different the morning was. It even smelled different, fresh, like new beginnings. Which was exactly what today was.

She could hear the traffic traveling down Congress Street, people heading to work. The birds were busy too, if the amount of noise they were generating from the trees in the neighborhood were any indication. For once, Carly had nowhere to rush off to, and the feeling was unnerving.

She did have plans to meet with Emily later that afternoon to discuss plans for the café. In their last text, Emily had again stated her excitement at the possibility of opening for Downtown Alive and Art Walk. Emily had said they would need a good bartender those nights, as the place would be crowded and needed someone with skills and a great personality.

Carly glared at the pink journal on the table. Now she had the time to write, but her muse remained silent. She needed something to get her mojo back. It seemed she'd been writing the same old thing for years. *How to Find a Boyfriend.* Well, now Joey wanted her, and she wanted Joey, but life just sucked sometimes. Somehow, Carly didn't think that would make the best of titles. No Amazon orange flag on that one.

The door opened to the little house next door, and Gibson came out to collect his morning paper. When he spotted her up on the porch, he waved.

"Good morning!"

"Mornin'!" Carly replied.

He tucked the newspaper under his arm and walked over to the stairs. Carly motioned him up with a wave of her hand.

"It's a gorgeous morning," he said as he took the other chair. "You can hardly tell that a few days ago, a crazy storm blew through the area."

Carly flinched. Had it only been a few days since her world tilted on its axis?

Gibson continued, and for that, Carly was grateful. "It does seem, though, that the storm blew in a new resident. How is Lafayette treating you so far?"

She thought of the days she'd spent in bed binge watching TV and feeling sorry for herself. Then she thought of the day before, spending the day on the basin with Lucky, the food, and the conversation.

"It's been good. Lucky was here yesterday. We went out to the Atchafalaya, and he did some fishing. I just took in the sights."

"That sounds like a great day."

"It really was," she admitted. "It was nice to just relax. And Lucky is a great cook."

"It's nice to see you getting out and seeing some sights. What do you have planned for lunch?"

The older gentleman was easy to talk to, almost like Daniel. "I'm meeting Emily at the café. We're going to talk plans and that stuff." She looked down at the still blank journal. "Then I may try getting some words down on paper."

"A writer, huh?"

She blushed and looked down. "Trying to be. Not being too successful so far."

"There are a couple who hang out at Legends in the afternoons. If you'd like, you can meet me there after you meet with Emily, and I'll introduce you."

"Really?"

"Yes. One is a published poet, and one writes these paranormal things with vampires and such."

Carly's eyes widened. "Vampires?"

"Yes, something about a haunted hotel in New Orleans. Not my thing, really, but they sell well."

"I have to meet this person."

"Okay, how about I come meet you at the café after lunch, then we can pop in."

"Sounds perfect, but I'm not sure how long things will take with Emily. How about a rain check for tomorrow?"

Gibson stood. "I'll see you then. I need to get back and get ready for the day. I have a few errands today now that everything seems to be up and running again."

"See you later, Gibson." Carly stood as well. She could smell the coffee through the open door and decided to go in and try round two.

She poured another cup and added a bit of half and half. She took a sip and smiled. The coffee was perfect.

Today was going to be a good day after all.

• • • •

CARLY STEPPED INTO the grocery store with no idea what of what she needed. Her normal trips included canned soups, diet frozen meals, and alcohol. She was determined to cook, though, so she was leaving with something. Taking a hard right, she passed down the bread aisle. She picked up a fresh loaf of soft French bread. One couldn't go wrong with that, right? It went with so many Cajun dishes.

The next meal in her new place would be one she made with her own hands.

Passing through the vegetable aisle, she picked up a container of pre-chopped onions, bell peppers, and celery. Although she may not be a cook, she'd watched Emily, Joey, and Glinda enough to know these three things were necessary.

Roaming through the store, she picked up various and random things. More coffee, Community, of course, cheeses, meats, some canned soups, and eggs. Passing the Cajun seasoning section, she spied a large container of spaghetti sauce. She picked up the jar and read the directions.

Brown one and a half pounds of ground meat. Add contents and some water. Simmer for 20-30 minutes. Serve over pasta.

"I can do this," she muttered aloud and put the jar in with her other items in the basket. "Jesus Christ, ground beef is high," she complained as she grabbed two plastic covered trays. "I could order out with what this costs."

After that, she added two bags of spaghetti and replaced the French bread with a loaf of garlic bread. Feeling pretty proud of herself, she smiled and headed to the front.

On her way to the check-out line, she passed through the baking section. She smiled as she passed the No-Bake Cheesecake. Thinking of past conversations with friends when they'd used cheesecake as a euphemism for sex, she grabbed a box. After reading the ingredients, she saw it had,, like three steps, only two if she bought the pre-made crust, which she would do. She nodded. She could do that. After one last pass through the store, she had all the ingredients, and a plan.

Considering the status of her love life, this would be the only cheesecake she would be getting.

• • • •

CARLY SIPPED HER TEA and opened her journal with a smile. Had it really been written only been a few days since she'd seen Jack again at the party? It already seemed like a lifetime ago, and maybe it was.

Speaking of food and eating (un)healthy, I think it's time to talk about cheesecake. One day, a group of friends and I were sitting around eating lunch and talking about men and dating. Someone had brought cheesecake for our dessert, and we decided cheesecake would be a great euphemism for sex. Well, it started out as sex, but we eventually expanded it to encompass an entire relationship.

There are different kinds of cheesecake, as there are different kinds of relationships. For example, there's No-Bake Cheesecake. It's cheap and easy to put together. It's for those people, like Jack, who don't want to put forth effort into making a relationship. He wants quick and easy with no hassle and no complications.

I am looking for gourmet cheesecake. I want top-of-the-line, exquisite cheesecake. The kind it takes effort and time to create. From the crust to the topping, everything works together for that perfect combination. That No-Bake can stay on the shelf, for all I care.

She closed the journal with a sigh. She had hoped that a read-through would give her some ideas to write about. But...nothing. Maybe meeting the writers later would give her a spark. How could she write about dating, or her love life, when both were the last thing on her mind?

The entry hadn't sent her into a tailspin again, like she had feared. Perhaps that was because she was already in a tailspin. New place, new job, new possibilities. Hard for the past to rock your world when the present had already done it for you.

• • • •

CARLY REACHED OUT FOR him, her smile captivating, welcoming. Joey took her hand and pulled her close, enjoying the feel of her against him, so perfect. Her citrusy shampoo drifted up and mixed with the clean scent of salt water. It drove him half wild. He fought for control.

She placed her hand on his face, her blue eyes beseeching. "I love you, Joey."

"I love..."

Eyes wide, Joey sat up in bed. Alone. He looked at his phone, hoping for a message from her, and was disappointed when the only messages were from Noah and Ryder. Frustrated, he threw the blankets aside and climbed out of bed.

He padded through the house, pausing by Carly's empty room. There was no sound coming from it. No TV left on, no Sammy snoring, nothing but silence. Combined with the silence of the island after the storm, it was eerie, almost haunting. Even the birds were quiet.

He shook it off and continued to the kitchen. He started a pot of coffee and turned the news on, thankful the electricity had been restored. He wondered what it was like in Lafayette. He would ask Noah later. He would know; Emily would tell him. She was coming by soon to pick up some things for Carly before heading out to Lafayette.

As was his habit, he set a frying pan on the stove and walked over to the fridge to retrieve some bacon. Opening the package, he automatically pulled out enough slices for himself, Carly, and a couple for Miss Sammy. With a sigh, he shoved over half back into the package. Breakfast alone. That didn't happen often. It had become routine for him to have breakfast with Carly. To talk about the day's events, the news, and get the day started. He missed seeing her messy blonde hair and sleepy eyes across the kitchen bar from him. The bacon started sizzling and began filling the house with its smell.

"Nothing smells better than bacon cooking in the morning," Joey said, repeating what Carly was in the habit of saying.

He listened as the newscasters out of New Orleans gave the news and weather while the coffee pot chugged along. There was no forecast for the storm he was facing.

• • • •

EMILY WAS BUSY WHEN Carly got to the café and didn't see her walk in, so Carly took a moment to look around. Emily had done well with the place. It was small but homey. Tables were scattered around the dining area in comfortable arrangements. It wasn't crowded or cluttered. Colorful local art adorned the walls.

On the back wall above the counter, there was a large piece of cypress with the words "*Bienvenue* to the Cypress Café" painted in large, ornate black letters.

Emily spotted her and made her way to Carly.

"How are you doing?" she asked after a welcome hug.

Carly nodded. "I'm okay. The first couple of days were rough."

"I understand. Look, I brought the things you needed from Joey's. I can drop them off at the apartment later."

"Awesome. Thank you so much. Oooh! I got the stuff to make spaghetti, if you want to stick around. I'll cook."

"You're going to cook?" Emily raised an eyebrow.

"Yes. With your help. You did say you would help me."

"Oh, girl. Of course. Wine?"

"You know it."

Emily grinned. "It's a plan. For now, let me show you around. You can meet Debra and Chantelle. After that, we can sit and talk, have some lunch. I'm sure you are starving."

Carly laughed. "I could use a good meal."

Emily took Carly through the building, showing her where everything was and describing how a typical day would go. It really wasn't that different from running a bar. There was daily stocking, cleaning, and housekeeping responsibilities.

"That's all there is to it," Emily said as they ended in the kitchen. "Grab a drink and have a seat, and I'll bring us both a plate."

Carly took a seat by the window, so she could watch the people pass by. It was mostly businessmen in their suits rushing to and from work and on errands. A man had set up across the street with a guitar, playing music and hoping for a few tips in his open instrument case.

Emily returned with plates of food that she set in front of both of them before sitting down.

"Lafayette is a lot different than Bon Chance." Carly waved a hand toward the busy street.

"Yes, it is, but I think you'll like it here."

"I think so too." The pace was busier than Bon Chance, but not as crazy as Houston had been when she lived there.

As they ate, they continued to chat about the café. "Downtown Alive and Art Walk are this weekend. It will be a great time for you to get a feel for the event and what local businesses do. I've booked a room for Noah and myself not far from here. I thought we'd come up and spend the weekend. You and I can brainstorm. Noah will probably want to bring up some of the new stock he's made. He's been busy the last few days helping people on the island with repairs. I'm sure he could use a couple days off."

Carly thought about the pieces she'd seen in the back room. Her brother had a definite talent for woodworking. His designs were simple, functional, and classic. He really should have the extra time to work on his passion and not worry about the day-to-day repairs at Snapper's.

"That sounds good. And Joey?" Carly asked.

"He talked about coming too."

Carly's heart skipped a little beat, thinking of seeing him again. With the excitement came a nervousness she knew would only grow in the next few days. Of course, he would be coming. What would keep him in Bon Chance? There was no Snapper's.

"It's a plan," Carly said. "I'm looking forward to it." And she meant it. Ryder was right. It was high time she got out of that bar and into her life.

Later, Carly rummaged through the white-framed glass cabinets looking for a wine glass. After pushing a few drinking glasses and Mardi Gras throw cups, she exclaimed, "A-ha!"

She laughed as she read some of the colorful quotes scrolling on the glasses.

"'Besties before testes.' Yeah, that doesn't work for me. Most of my besties have testes." She reached for another one. "'Hocus Pocus, I need wine to focus.' Not quite Halloween yet." The next one had a corkscrew and the words *Screw This*.

Carly nodded and grabbed that one. "Perfect. Which one do you want, Emily?" Emily then rummaged through the collection, choosing one with a big yellow and black bee and the word *Buzzed*. "Gemma definitely has a sense of humor."

Emily took a seat at the small round table in the middle of the kitchen. "This is nice. All I have to do is supervise."

Carly laughed out loud. "You may be cooking by the time this is all said and done."

"Nonsense. You've got this."

"Thank you again for bringing up my stuff. I just don't know if I'm ready to see Snapper's yet."

"It's not a problem. I don't mind. However, when I stopped by, Joey looked like he didn't quite know what to do with himself with you gone."

"Poor Joey. I miss him. I think Sammy does too. She misses her morning bacon." As if the dog understood, she slapped her tail on the floor a few times.

"He mentioned coming up this weekend. I think it would be good. Maybe y'all can go on that date?" Emily winked.

Carly dodged the question, gesturing instead to the pan on the stove. "Do you think I should do anything else right now?"

"No, just stir it every now and then, keep breaking up the ground beef. And you didn't answer my question. Ooooh, you could cook spaghetti for him when he comes over. Woo him with your culinary skills."

Carly rolled her eyes. "That's your department. I'll probably trip over something and fall into his arms."

"Hey, now! That's a thought. All you need to do is put on some heels. I can bring some up before he comes. You can pretend to fall, and he can be your hero."

"Pretend? You've seen me in heels, right?"

"Of course I have. That's what makes this perfect."

Carly turned to check on the food again. "Should I turn the fire up?"

"You can if you want. You'll just need to keep an eye on it, so it doesn't burn. Or you can leave it lower. It will take a bit longer to cook, but I've got nothing but time right now. And this conversation is intriguing me."

"You're messy, Emily."

Emily took a sip of wine. "Oh, come on, Carly, this has gone on long enough. It's gotten almost painful to watch."

"Do you have to be so honest?"

"Of course I do." She burst out in song. "That's what friends are for..."

Carly rolled her eyes. "I'm going to take a picture of this and send to Joey. He's not going to believe it." She grabbed her camera and took a snap of the skillet with the slowly browning beef.

"I love this song!" Emily exclaimed as the beginning melody of an Aaron Lewis song started to play from the small speaker they had linked to Carly's phone. "I always think of this as Noah's and my song."

"*Tangled up in You*? It's such a pretty song. And it fits. Oh, and how are things with you and my brother? Thinking about taking a trip down the aisle any time soon?"

"I think we're perfectly content at the moment."

"Aw, man, I want some nieces or nephews."

"You have Oscar." At the sound of his name, he raised his big head from his spot on the floor.

"That's not quite what I meant."

"Anyway, what's it looking like over there? It's smelling like it's about ready."

"It's brown."

"Awesome. Let's drain the grease off, and then all we have to do is add the sauce and boil some noodles. Look how easy."

Carly soon had everything going again. "This is kind of soothing," she said as she stirred the dark red sauce that was slowly beginning to bubble up. "I see why you like cooking so much."

"Right? One of these days we'll tackle a fettuccini or gumbo. Gumbo is easy, but you better be ready to make a lot. I've never figured out how to make a small one."

"I've never seen a small gumbo."

Carly stirred the sauce again, inhaling the spicy scent and smiling. "I gotta send another pic." She reached for her phone. "Oh, crap. My battery is getting low. Let me go grab my charger really quick." Carly went to the bedroom and grabbed the charger. When she got back the sauce was bubbling faster.

"You might want to turn that down," Emily said.

Carly reached out to lower the fire, and as she did, a huge bubble formed, and red sauce went everywhere. All over Carly's shirt, the oven, and even small red dots on the ceiling.

"Damn!" she exclaimed, holding her hand out where some of the liquid had splashed, scalding her.

As she ran her hand under the faucet, letting the cold water soothe her, Emily took over, wiping everything down and stirring the sauce.

The stinging subsided, and she turned and leaned against the counter. She took a sip of her wine and exhaled. "Nice. See, this is why I don't cook."

Oscar rose from his spot and trotted over to Carly. He stood on his hind legs, sniffing the spots where the sauce had landed. When he started licking her shirt, she laughed and pushed him gently back to the floor.

"Go away, Oscar."

"Are you going to live?" Emily asked, shooing the dog away and handing Carly a dish towel.

"Maybe," Carly said, twisting her lips into a pout, then threw back her head and laughed. "Get outta the way. I have a meal to finish."

Chapter Eleven

THE NEXT AFTERNOON, Carly stepped into the kitchen of the Cypress Café and switched the lights on. She picked up the to-do list Emily had left for her yesterday. Her heart skipped a beat. She didn't feel nearly as confident as she had the day before. Debra would be here soon, and she would know what to do.

It can't be that difficult. Not that much different than Snapper's. Only with food. But Joey had taken care of all that. He would have had a conniption if she had even attempted to help him out.

She smiled a little at that thought. He was so OCD about this kitchen. She often went in and moved things a bit when he wasn't looking just to get a rise out of him.

Sitting there in the quiet, dark room, Carly could close her eyes and imagine she was in was Snapper's. The lingering smells of food and cleaning supplies mingled together just as they had when she had opened the bar.

Not anymore. The was no bar, no Snapper's, no Joey. Her heart constricted, and a tear slipped down her cheek. She sat on one of the stools by the large window that faced Jefferson Street.

Light flashed into the dark room, and Carly glanced over expecting to see Debra, but instead saw Lucky. He clicked on the lights.

"You always like to sit in the dark?" he asked.

She wiped away a tear. "I just haven't gotten that far yet."

He reached out and tucked a finger under her chin. "Aw, *cher*, opening a kitchen can't be that hard."

Carly laughed. "I'm sure. What are you doing here, by the way?"

"I was just passing by. I have a reno just down the street, remember?"

"Oh, yeah."

He pointed to the clipboard in her hand. "Lemme see that."

She handed it to him, and he looked it over for a moment. "Oh, *cher*, come on. I got you covered."

Carly watched as Lucky moved around the kitchen like he belonged there. Was there anywhere this guy felt uncomfortable or out of place? Probably in a tuxedo. He looked like the type who would pull at the collar, and long to take the jacket off and roll up the sleeves.

Carly thought of those muscular arms wrapped up in a white dress shirt, sleeves up, and her throat went dry.

"I'm here!" Debra announced as she walked into the kitchen. "Well, Lucky LeBlanc, what are you doing in here?"

"I felt like stirring up a little somethin' before work." He winked at Carly.

"I never complain when I see a handsome man in the kitchen."

He wrapped the woman in a hug. "And I love a hot woman in the kitchen."

"If by hot you mean from the heat in the room, you got that right."

"Aw, now, Ms. Debra, you are a beautiful woman."

She hit him with the dish towel she was cleaning with. "No, go on. We got work to do, and you're distracting us."

Lucky grinned. "Bye, ladies. I'll be back later for one of your awesome plate lunches." He tipped the brim of his baseball cap before leaving them in the kitchen.

Monica was next to arrive, and she soon had Carly too busy and distracted to think about Snapper's.

Monica rattled off a list of things for Carly to do, and she hustled to follow the directions.

"Stir this."

"Add to this pot."

"Chop these vegetables. No, not like that. Like this." Monica took a moment to show Carly how to dice the ingredients they would need to cook with.

The kitchen was soon filled with wonderful aromas of soups and sauces bubbling in the big gray pots.

Chantelle, the waitress, arrived next, and her quiet but efficient manner as she readied the dining room was a complement to Debra's more exuberant one.

Carly had one moment to take a breath, then the kitchen opened for lunch. That was the last moment of rest she would have.

• • • •

AFTER WORK, CARLY FOLLOWED Gibson down Jefferson Street toward Legends. While they walked, he gave her tidbits of trivia about the local businesses and parks.

"This is a new pizza place. It opened about a year ago. They have this wonderful New York style pizza. And look at their outdoor eating place. It's a parking spot. Some of the business are doing this. They're called parklets."

Carly looked at the few patrons seated in the small area enjoying some sunshine. "That's cool."

"You'll be checking out Downtown Alive tomorrow night?" Gibson asked.

"I will. Emily and Noah are coming as well." *And Joey.*

"You'll love the band. It's a local swamp pop band that will have you dancing all night long."

"Not me so much," Carly said. "You saw me the other day."

"We'll change that. I'm sure we can find some young guy to show you the ropes."

"We'll see. We'll see." She laughed.

Daniel stopped in front of one business. "We're here. Now, the interesting part about this place is that there are actually two Legends. There's this one," he held the door open for Carly, "then there's the annex that's just across the way."

It was bigger on the inside than it looked on the outside, the whole room ran what seemed to be half the block. A long white bar ran most of the length, illuminated from underneath with neon blue lighting.

"Since it's a pretty day, most of the regulars are probably outside," Gibson said as they walked up to the bar where the bartender slid a glass in front of him.

"Hello, Gibson," she greeted. The woman was packed with a lot of personality, according to the tattoos she had decorating her body. The faces of Lily Munster and Lucille Ball were on one arm. But the one that really caught Carly's attention was the words "Semper Fi" scrolling across her chest.

"Hi! What can I get for you?" she asked.

Gibson said, "Whatever she's having is on me. This is Carly. She's relocating to Lafayette for the time being, and I'm showing her the sights. Carly, this is Lily."

"It's nice to meet you," Lily said.

"You too. A Marine, huh? My brother is a Marine."

"Semper Fi," Lily said, flexing a muscle. "It's awesome to have you here in our town. I'm sure you will love it. Now, what are you having today?"

Carly told her what she wanted, and Lily went to retrieve her order.

When Carly had her beer, Gibson said, "Are you ready to go meet the others?"

"Sure."

They stepped out of the dark bar into the bright sunshine, and Carly had to blink a few times as they adjusted. Scattered around the patio area were assorted black wrought iron tables and chairs mixed in with wooden patio tables. Bright pink flowers poured from hanging baskets.

A small group of people sat around two of the wrought iron tables. She followed Gibson, and he began making introductions.

"Carly, this is Patricia." A petite woman with shoulder length curly brown hair raised her pink koozie.

"The Pink Pony," Carly said, mentioning a popular bar on the Alabama coast. "I've been there a time or two."

"Good times!" Patricia said.

"This is Dylan. Our resident poet." A handsome, dark-haired guy who looked to be in his forties raised an Abita bottle.

"And Dawn, she's the one I told you about."

The brown-haired woman with a ponytail and wearing jeans and a t-shirt winked. "All good, I hope."

"Carly here wants to write a book."

"Awesome. Pull up a chair, Carly," Dawn said. Carly took the empty seat next to Dylan.

"Where are you from, Carly?" Patricia asked.

"Bon Chance."

"Aw, man. Didn't they get hit pretty heavy in the storm?"

The words lanced through her. She wondered if it would get easier. She twirled the beer in front of her and peeled at the label.

"Carly, tell us about what you want to write," Dawn said, saving her from having to reply to the Snapper's conversation.

"I'm not sure. I wrote a little romance thing, more of a journal. I've tried to get it published, but no one's grabbed it yet. What about you? What do you write? Gibson said something about vampires?"

"I write the *Chateau Rouge* books. They're about a haunted hotel in New Orleans."

Carly's eyes widened, "No way! I love those books! You're Ivy Rose?"

Dawn blushed. "Yes. That's me."

"OhmyGod!"

"Looks like you have a fan, Dawn," Gibson said.

"At least one." Dawn laughed.

Carly had so many questions jam in her head, she couldn't speak. Ivy Rose. In front of her. She didn't want to impose, though. She had only just met the woman.

"I'm between manuscripts right now. If you'd like me to take a look at yours, let me know."

Carly's eyes went wide. "I would love it."

"Cool deal. Bring it when you're ready. You can find me here most days. If the writing went well in the morning, that is."

Usually the talkative one, Carly was too dumbfounded to talk much after that. She was content to listen to the conversation around her. Just wait until she told Joey! And Ryder!

. . . .

JOEY POPPED THE TOP off a beer and sat down on the wooden steps of the Redbird. Daniel and Glinda were still in San Antonio, spending time with Gabriel and Grace. He and Noah had just finished repairing a window that had been broken in the storm.

Noah followed suit. "Windows replaced. Electricity restored on the island. This place will be up and running soon."

"There's no rush for Aunt Glinda to come back. The tourism will be slow until everything gets close to back to normal."

"I agree. She needs a little break, anyway."

Noah grinned. "Maybe she and Daniel are having some alone time."

"Lord knows he's been trying to get her to be more serious." Joey laughed.

"Sounds like someone else I know."

Joey tossed the bottlecap he'd been toying with into the trash, "I don't know, Noah. This storm has messed up more than Snapper's. Now we aren't even in the same town anymore. The house is so quiet without her. I almost thought of rescuing a dog the other day just because I miss that damn grumpy dog of hers so much."

"You should. And you should come with us to see Carly this weekend. You know, it may be different. It doesn't have to be romantic. You two are still friends."

"I know, but she's going through so much. It doesn't seem fair to say, 'Hey, Carly, let's try to see where this can go,' when everything is so messed up."

"I get that. But she loves you. She does, in her own way. The best thing is to do what you've always done. Be her friend."

"I always will be. I just wish she knew that."

"She knows, my friend. She knows." Noah reached out and clinked his bottle to Joey's. "Just hang in there."

Joey's phone pinged, and he looked down. "Speak of the devil." He took a second to read the text. "Well, I'll be damned."

"What is it?"

"She met some kind of author. Wants to see her writing."

"Isn't that something?" Noah winked at Joey. "Looks like we have something to celebrate this weekend."

"I think we do. Looks like we're heading to Lafayette tomorrow."

Chapter Twelve

AFTER HER SECOND SHIFT at the café, Carly had come home, showered, and taken a nap. The lunch shift had been steady and busy. There was always an order to take or deliver, or a table to wipe down. Fridays were even busier than the previous day. Seemed everyone in the downtown area wanted to get out and eat lunch. No wonder Emily wanted to expand to opening for events like the ones they were going to that weekend. The extra business would make her café even more profitable.

Now Carly sat outside on the porch in the rocking chair, sipping a beer. Emily had sent her a text earlier. They would be there in about half an hour. Emily said they would just park at the apartment and walk. It would be easier that way. After walking around downtown the last couple of days and noticing the lack of parking, Carly could see why.

Sammy sat on the top of the porch steps, watching for intruders. Occasionally, she would bark at passersby but wouldn't move.

Carly thought of Emily when she had returned to Bon Chance after leaving Eddie. She had been so quiet, even more so than Carly remembered from high school. It was like the life had been sucked out of her. But she had slowly warmed up again, especially with Noah. It had been something to watch the light return to both their eyes.

Such a sweet love story.

The kind people wrote books about.

Carly felt the buzz of inspiration and quickly grabbed the ever-present journal beside her and jotted a few notes.

Friends to lovers?

Second chances?

Coming home?

She tapped the pen against her lips, trying to think of characters for the story, but the images of Emily and Noah kept popping into her head.

"That's not working," she muttered, putting the notebook away.

At that time, Noah's truck turned into her driveway. He and Emily climbed out, waving as they walked up.

"How was today?" Emily asked as she took a seat in the wooden rocking chair.

Carly smiled. "Busy. Very busy."

"Good. I'm sure the ladies were helpful."

"Very much so. I think they could have actually run the place without me." Carly laughed.

"Me too. They are awesome."

"Where's Joey?" Carly asked, not seeing his Jeep.

Noah responded, "He's coming. He wanted to make a stop along the way. He won't be long."

"Oh, good. I'm looking forward to tonight, actually. Everyone was talking about the band playing tonight. They're supposed to be a lot of fun."

"That's good." Emily looked at Noah. "If it gets to be too much, we can always go to Gemma's or even the café."

He smiled at Emily, reaching out to kiss her softly. "I'll be fine." When Noah had returned from Iraq, he had suffered from PTSD, and crowds or loud noises could trigger panic attacks. His service dog, Sadie, had been a big help, and so had Emily's always calm presence. It was like he found a sense of peace when he was with her.

"Hey, y'all want a beer?" Carly asked.

"Yeah, that would be great," Noah said. "The traffic was terrible on the Thruway."

"It always is," Emily said.

Carly went back into the apartment and snagged three beers out of the fridge. She was ready for another one as well. She had just handed Emily and Noah theirs and sat down when Joey rounded the corner.

With both spots taken in the driveway, he drove up a bit and parked on the curb. Carly's heart started beating faster as the driver's side opened.

Joey was here. She stood in greeting as he turned her way. His normal shorts and t-shirts had been replaced with jeans and a black polo. Her knees went weak when he smiled. She reached out to the rocking chair for support and cursed when it swayed with her weight.

He walked up the steps with a bright red gift bag in one hand. "I hear a celebration is in order," he said, handing the bag to Carly.

"A celebration?" she asked, puzzled. "What is there to celebrate?"

"You met a writer who wants to read your work. That sounds like something to me."

"Oh, yes! Definitely. I haven't given her my stuff yet. I'm so nervous. What if she hates it?"

"What if she likes it?" Joey asked.

"I don't want to think about any of that yet."

He nudged her. "Well, go on, open it."

She pulled the sparkly white gift paper out and reached down into the bag. She lifted out a bottle of champagne. "Nice!" she exclaimed. "My favorite."

There was something else in the bag, so she reached down into it again, pulling out a wire bound journal.

The cover was painted in rainbow shades and the words "Writing is the painting of the voice—Voltaire" scrolled across in gold letters.

"Oh, Joey!" she said, clasping the book to her chest.

He smiled. "New journal? New writing?"

She jumped up out of the chair to hug him. She inhaled the familiar scent of him, spicy and woodsy, and utterly appealing. He held for a moment then slowly pulled away.

"Thank you," she said. "It's perfect."

"You're very welcome. Now, I hear there's some kind of thing going on tonight. Y'all ready to head that way? I'm starving."

Noah and Emily finished off their beers and tossed them in the small trashcan in the corner. "Let's go. The night is young, and so are we."

They heard the music a couple of blocks before they made it to Parc Sans Souci, the smaller venue downtown. They stopped near the water fountain and watched as kids splashed around and Joey ordered some food from one of the vendors.

Noah went for drinks while the ladies waited.

"That's some present Joey brought you," Emily said.

"It was. I'm so lucky to have him for a friend."

Emily smiled. "I'm not saying anything tonight."

Carly made a face. "Thank you. Let me just enjoy this."

"I will, my friend. Tonight, let's have a good time and forget about everything else."

Joey returned shortly after Noah with a small white bowl of jambalaya. He munched away on it as they continued walking closer to the raised gazebo where the band played. They stopped at the outskirts of the crowd, careful not to get too close and make Noah uncomfortable.

"That was good," Joey said as he finished off the rice and meat dish. "Not as good as mine, of course, but still good." He tossed the empty bowl into the nearest trash bin.

Carly jumped, feeling a swat on her behind. Then she heard the familiar Ryder growl in her ear. She rolled her eyes and turned to hug him.

"What are you doing here?" she asked when she stepped back.

He put his hands on his latest belt buckle win. "They're having a bull riding tournament at The Broken Spoke this weekend. I thought I'd come check it out."

"Bull riding? In a bar in Lafayette?"

"The bull's mechanical. But the pretty ladies who will be there are very real."

Carly shook her head. "You're incorrigible."

"I'm not sure what that means, but if it means irresistible, you are right."

The band was playing a lively Cajun tune, and Ryder took her hand and spun her around. "You are looking pretty yourself tonight, Carly. This town looks good on you."

She grinned. "Thank you, Ryder."

He spun her around again. "Now, I'm going to go find me a good dance partner."

She pushed him toward the dance floor. "Go, then."

He blew her a kiss. "See you in a bit."

He disappeared into the crowd of people. Carly was sure she would see him scooting some good-looking woman around the dance area in a matter of moments.

Joey returned to her side, close but not too close, and for that, Carly was grateful. The space was appreciated so she could relax and simply enjoy the evening.

The sun was slowly beginning to set, casting soft orange light across the park. The band began a slow Cajun waltz, *Pieces to My Heart*.

"Dance with me," Carly said to Joey, holding out her hand.

"Of course." He took her hand and led her through the crowd of people and out to the dance area in front of the band.

Once there, he placed his hands on her hips. She, in turn, put hers on his shoulders. Slowly, they swayed to the music just like they had probably a hundred times before.

It was so normal, and so right.

She leaned closer to him and rested her head on his chest. He missed a step, but quickly recovered. He kissed the top of her head, and Carly smiled.

For a moment, this was all she needed.

• • • •

JOEY BREATHED IN THE citrusy scent of Carly, forcing his body to calm down. Damn it! Why did a hurricane have to come and mess things up? He thought of their kiss in the rain. Wondered what she would do if he kissed her tonight like he wanted to. Would it scare her away? And what next? Nothing was the same as it had been only a few days ago.

Honestly, it felt like starting all over again. Not only with Carly, but with his own life. He had changes he needed to make. He needed to find a new place to live if he was going to school in New Orleans. Then get moved. Had to get enrolled first. His to-do list seemed to grow daily.

Carly snuggled in closer to him, and he hugged her tighter. All thoughts of the future and New Orleans disappeared. For now, this was enough. He had all weekend to take his time and just enjoy being with her. Maybe a little brunch in the morning with some mimosas? A leisurely stroll through downtown?

The song was over entirely too soon for Joey, and they were walking back to Noah and Emily. Ryder had returned as well. Slow songs that early in the night were not his thing.

"Need another?" Joey asked Carly, who nodded. He surveyed the rest of the group. "Anyone else?"

He took note of the responses and left to find the nearest beer tent. It didn't take too long, and he was purchasing a round and heading back to the group.

When he got back, someone else had joined them. Someone very familiar to Ryder and Carly, judging by the way he was standing so close to the two of them.

The guy leaned in and said something to Carly, making her laugh, a blush spreading across her face.

Joey's stomach tightened. It was the first time in a while that he had seen a stranger flirt with her, and her return the attention. The last time was Jack, and she had fallen hard for him. It had taken her months to recover from that infatuation.

Joey inhaled. What if, after all this time, she fell for someone else?

He brushed that thought away as he walked up to Carly.

"Here you go," he said as he handed her the cold beverage. She took it, discarding the empty and replacing the fresh in her koozie.

"Thank you." She gestured toward New Guy. "This is Lucky Leblanc. A Leblanc, and yes, this is a cousin of Ryder's."

Joey held out his hand. "Hi, Lucky. It's nice to meet you."

"You too. Any friend of Ryder's is a friend of mine. I've known Emily for a good bit too. My brother's company did the reno on her café." Lucky was so genuinely friendly it was hard to not like him.

"I'm trying to talk him into riding the bull tonight," Ryder said.

"I keep telling him that I don't ride things intent on bucking me off and killing me." He grinned, his blue eyes sparkling.

Definitely Ryder's cousin. Would that charm work on Carly? Carly, the queen of bad decisions when she was upset, especially when men were involved. This had disaster written all over it.

The music switched to a Cajun waltz, and Lucky reached out for Carly's hand. "I know you can do this one. Anyone can do three steps and a spin."

"Actually, I can do this one. It's the only one."

"Come on and dance with me, *cher*." He leered at Carly, and Joey felt that same sinking in his gut that only increased when she followed him out onto the dance floor.

"You know she's crazy about you, don't you?" Ryder said when they were out of earshot.

"It doesn't look like it."

"Why don't you just make a move?"

"It's not that simple."

"It is," Ryder disagreed.

"She's not interested in that right now. She's going through a lot."

"Yes, she is. And you can be there for her."

"I always will."

"Joey, you can be her friend and her lover too. What's going to happen the next time there's a crisis? Would you break up with her when times get rough?"

"Of course not."

"Then stop making excuses. Ask her out. Life's too short." Ryder's eyes darkened, and Joey wondered what had caused the pain the look implied. Ryder was right, though. It was time for Joey to do something, before Carly did more than dance away with another man.

Chapter Thirteen

CARLY AWOKE TO THE sun streaming through the sheer white curtains. She definitely missed her blackout curtains at home. She loved her Bat Cave, and the fact that she could take a nap at any point during the day. Working nights for so long, it was important to sleep in until well after the sun had risen.

Times there were a changin', though, and now she woke up with the chickens, or roosters, or whatever that was making noise outside. She stretched and looked around when she realized Sammy was not at the foot of the bed. She went into the living room.

Joey was curled up on the small sofa, his legs hanging over the side. Sammy was feet up under his arm.

"Bitch," she whispered. For a moment, she imagined it was her under Joey's arm, all warm next to him. Her body heated, especially her lady parts.

She shook the feeling off and went in the kitchen to start a pot of coffee. She was going to need all the stamina she could get today to ward off her feelings for her best friend.

While the coffee brewed, she brushed her teeth and traded her Frankenstein leggings for blue jeans. When she returned to the kitchen, Joey had woken up. His blanket was folded and resting on the arm of the chair. Judging by the open door, he had gone outside, probably to let Sammy out.

She checked on the coffee. It had finished, so she poured herself and Joey a cup. She added a liberal amount of cream to her own, then carried the mugs out to the porch.

Joey raised an eyebrow when she set his mug down beside him. "Coffee?"

"Yes, it took me a few tries, but I think I make a reasonable cup now."

He raised the mug to his lips, sniffing it first. "It doesn't smell too bad."

"How can coffee smell bad?" she asked.

Joey took a sip. "Not bad. I'm impressed."

"See?"

"I'm interested in seeing what else you're good at,"

He set the mug down and reached for her hand. He picked it up and kissed the palm. When she shivered, she heard the groan he tried to hide. "I know it's not dancing,"

"True. I doubt I ever master that."

"Well, dancing queen, what would you like to do with your day today? Art Walk isn't until later this evening. Emily and Noah are working at the café. Anything around here you would like to do? Brunch?"

"That would be great. I hear they have a place not far from here that serves a great one. With mimosas and everything."

"Sounds like a plan to me. Want the bathroom first?"

"Oh, yeah. I know it's going to take you, like, five minutes to get ready." She rolled her eyes.

"Hey, it gives me more time to drink this awesome coffee you made." He winked as he took another sip.

She felt the blush rise on her cheeks at his compliment. It wasn't often anyone said anything nice about anything she made in the kitchen. Lucky called her Super Woman and now Joey, the food snob, liked her coffee. She settled back into the rocking chair, feeling quite satisfied with herself. She could get used to this.

•   •   •   •

A HALF AN HOUR LATER, they were both ready and heading toward downtown. The mid-morning air was cool, just enough to need the hoodies they had donned before leaving the apartment. They made small talk as they walked, about the weird statues in front of the federal courthouse, the pair of heads that looked like they had been chopped off right above the forehead.

They passed the small park across the street from the courthouse that had brightly colored benches under the branches of tall trees.

It wasn't long, and they were walking up to Dwyer's Café, and it was already full of people. They declined a table, instead choosing to sit at the bar. Sports news was already on, talking about which college teams were going to win.

Carly ordered a mimosa while they perused the menu. "Everything looks so good."

"I think I'll have the cheeseburger omelet," Joey said.

"You and cheeseburgers," Carly said. "An omelet does sound good, though. Especially the spinach one."

The waitress came back, and they placed their orders and returned their menus.

Joey sipped on his bloody mary, spinning it around slowly on the bar. He was thinking about seeing Carly with Lucky the night before and his conversation with Ryder. Ryder had already sent him a text asking if he had followed through with his decision to ask Carly out.

"What's on your mind?" Carly asked.

"Let's go out tonight," he blurted.

She smiled. "We are. We're going to Art Walk."

"No, Carly," he reached for her hand, "let's go *out*."

"Ohhhh," her blue eyes widened, "like a date?"

He nodded.

"A for real date?"

He nodded again. His nerves were shot all to pieces as he waited for a yes or no.

She squeezed his hand that still covered hers. "Let's do it."

He took another sip of his drink to hide his breath of relief. "Awesome. We can go before Art Walk if you'd like. It would be a bit early."

"That's fine. I'd rather go before than after. That way we can enjoy the art, and Morgan says some places will have music. In fact, I think Gemma's is one of them."

"Great. It's a plan, then."

She grinned. "Yes, it is."

The waitress returned with their food, placing the dishes in front of them.

"This looks incredible," Carly said.

"It does," Joey agreed, gesturing down to the fluffy yellow omelet with a side of sliced red tomatoes. He nodded after the first bite. "Very good. I'm going to have to remember this idea. Speaking of ideas, let me know where you would like to go tonight. I have no clue where to go."

Carly frowned. "Me either. We can look when we get home." She stopped and looked down for a moment. "I mean the apartment. It's not really 'home.'"

It was his turn to reach out and squeeze her hand. "It *is* home. For now."

"You're right. Let's finish this meal, and we can get back *home* and figure out where to go."

Joey nodded, in complete agreement. He couldn't wait to see what the night would bring.

• • • •

CARLY LOOKED AT HERSELF again in the large oval full-length mirror. She turned this way and that way, not completely convinced her striped blue blouse and jeans were the right thing to wear on her first date with Joey. But with most of her wardrobe still in Bon Chance, she didn't have much choice.

Maybe I should have run to a store. Bought something else. She shook off the thought. This was Joey, who was used to seeing her in t-shirts and flip-flops. Just putting on two coats of mascara was dressed up for her.

She had been stunned when Joey actually asked her on the date. Every reason she could think of to turn him down ran through her head—bad timing, she wasn't ready, why mess things up with dating right now. But one look in those brown eyes of his, and she was nodding.

She took one last look in the mirror, breathing deeply to calm her nerves. She was going on a date. With Joey. Who was currently waiting on her to leave the bedroom so he could get ready. Carly could see why Gemma had moved in with Jasper. This apartment was way too small for two people.

She would slide on her sandals when Joey was ready. She took one more deep breath and opened the door.

Joey was on the couch, watching a football game. He looked up as the door opened. His dimpled grin was all she needed to see.

"You look great," he said.

"Thank you."

He stood, and Carly shifted from one foot to the other. This was beyond awkward. It wasn't even like she could wait for him to show up. He was already there. But if things were normal, it wouldn't be her life.

Sammy had taken up residence on the couch beside Joey, and Carly patted her on the head on her way to the kitchen.

She grabbed a beer out of the fridge, popped the top, and wandered out onto the front porch. She rocked softly, listening to the sound of the rocker as it moved. She could hear the traffic on Congress as it passed by.

She waved at Gibson as he walked toward his house.

"Are you going downtown?" he asked.

"Yes, we are. We're going out to eat first."

"Great! Where are you going?"

"Some place called The Little Big Cup."

"Oh, yeah. You're going to love it. It's right on the water. Food is great too."

"Nice."

"We'll catch up later."

Carly picked up her phone, scrolling through social media, trying to keep her mind off her date. What would it be like in the truck? Eating? Would he try to kiss her? Her stomach fluttered at the thought.

Everything was different now. They had crossed a line they had both resisted for so long.

Well, if everything changed, at least this change was positive. Hopefully.

• • • •

JOEY TOOK HIS TIME in the shower, his nerves getting the better of him. On one hand, he was going on a date with Carly. On the other, he was going on a date with Carly. The thought was both exciting and frightening. This was not a night with some stranger he met online or at Snapper's or anywhere else.

This was Carly, his best friend since forever.

Awkward didn't even begin to describe how he felt. Inwardly, he cursed Ryder. Why in the hell had he taken love advice from Ryder, of all people? He should have talked to Noah first, but he was Carly's brother, which was weird too.

It was too late to turn back now. He turned the water off. Ready or not, Little Big Cup here they came.

He took care to dress in a black oxford shirt, nice jeans, and loafers that hadn't been worn in probably two years. Not since he'd started cooking at Snapper's. Everything went casual then, t-shirts, jeans, ball caps. It was one thing he loved about running the kitchen there. Everything about it was comfortable. Perhaps too comfortable, and that was why he was just now taking the next step with Carly.

He splashed on a little bit of cologne, but not too much. They did have to ride together in the truck to the restaurant. He checked his hair one more time to make sure it wasn't poking up anywhere and took a deep breath.

If all went well, he'd have Carly in his arms when the night ended. He took a deep breath and went to find her.

• • • •

"OHMYGOD, JOEY! LOOK at this place!" Carly exclaimed as they walked through the very nondescript door into the restaurant. The middle room, the one they were in, was flanked by two smaller rooms, each separated by French doors. The main room was a huge, open area. Couples sat at the various tables, the women mostly sipping on drinks in varying shades of pastels and adorned with pieces of fruit.

Jazz music played softly through the speakers, just covering the ambient noise of the customers.

Carly reached for Joey's hand. "It's like stepping into someplace tucked away in the French Quarter. But bigger."

The hostess approached them, and Carly asked if they could be seated outside.

"Of course," she said. "Follow me."

Carly was thrilled when Joey hadn't released her hand. This really was like a real date. Her first real date in almost a year, and it was with Joey. Only a few months or even weeks ago, she never would have believed it.

The hostess showed them to their table, seating them beside the railing that overlooked the murky bayou.

"I can't believe how awesome this place is," Carly said. "And here in the middle of nowhere. I read they have a buffet on Sundays too. We should check that out one day."

"We can definitely see. We haven't had the food yet, though. What if it's terrible?" he teased.

"Then we'll just come drink and watch people. Look how the deck goes all the way to the water. We should take a walk after we eat."

Joey smiled. "You going to take your shoes off and let your legs dangle off the side? Like old times?"

She shuddered. "Not here. I don't know what's in that water."

"You didn't know what was in the water."

"I'm smarter now. I'm surprised a gator didn't bite my foot off."

"I doubt there were any gators lurking in that water." He nodded toward the bayou. "*That* water, probably gators. Maybe a snake or two."

Carly peered over the railing. "You think?"

"If there are, they are more scared of you than you are of them."

"Let's not think about that right now," she said, ready for a change of subject. She didn't want to spend their night talking about creepy crawlies.

The waitress came with their drinks, and after giving her their orders, Carly leaned back in her chair. She took a sip of the colorful drink she had ordered.

"This is amazing. I need to learn how to make it. I didn't have to make too many fancy drinks at Snapper's. It was pretty much beer or bourbon and Cokes."

"You know, you could come to New Orleans with me. I'm sure you'd get a variety of orders."

"It's so tempting, Joey." Carly thought of actually living in New Orleans and having the French Quarter in her back yard. Walking down Royal and looking at the antique stores. Or through Jackson Square and looking at all the art. The town screamed inspiration. "I bet I wouldn't get writer's block there."

"Why don't you come visit after I get moved in? We can go from there. You can check out the job scene."

"I like it here so far. It's so laidback."

"It's been, like, three days." Joey laughed.

"True. Let's just take this one day at a time."

"This?" He pointed to her then to himself. "Us? Or visiting?"

"Both."

"Is this Carly speaking? Miss Impulsive?"

"Maybe I'm finally growing up."

"I like it." His brown eyes softened as he looked at her, and her insides went all squishy. "I get it. One day at a time, it is."

It was his turn to lean back. "So, New Carly, what else would you like to do?"

"What do you mean?"

"Look at us. We're here. It's a Saturday night. When was the last time we were able to just sit back and relax on a Saturday? Since we opened Snapper's, our weekends have been full of bar stuff. Getting the kitchen ready, stocking, cooking, cleaning...the list goes on." He gestured around the restaurant. "When was the last time we got to sit and enjoy a meal that I didn't cook? A meal that we didn't discuss schedules and workers, and upcoming events?"

She sighed. "I couldn't tell you." He was right. The bar had consumed both their lives. Talk always centered about work. "So, let's not talk about that either."

"Okay, so no snakes and no Snapper's. Let's talk about what we can do with all this free time." The way he said *we* sent shivers up her spine. She could think of a thing or two they could do that had nothing to do with work.

"Cold?" he asked.

Her face grew warm, and she looked away, scared to meet his eyes. If he saw the truth, how much she wanted him, there would be no going back. She shook off her X-rated thoughts and focused on the question he had initially asked her.

"What do I want to do? I'd like to travel. I never really got far from Bon Chance. I went as far as Houston and Biloxi, and that was it. There's so much else to see, though. I'd like to go see Gabe and Grace in Austin. I've heard such awesome things about that town."

"That's definitely doable. I'd like to see that too, and San Antonio. The River Walk looks so cool."

Sitting there talking to him about the future seemed so natural, but everything did with Joey. It always had been. The tough part was making that jump from comfortable to intimate. Just what would she do when she woke up with him the next morning?

Damnit, there goes my mind again. Luckily, the waitress was there with their plates of food to occupy her mind.

She took a bite of her crab cake. "These are incredible! Here, you taste." She pushed her plate close to him so he could try.

"They are. What is that again?"

"Crab cakes and fried eggplant."

"Nice. I'm going to have to remember that."

"This is something you could never could have made for Snapper's," she said. "Just like me and the fancy drinks."

Comfortable. Snapper's had been comfortable. Like the perfect pair of worn-out jeans. Worn-out being the operative word. Carly looked from her drink to the elegant plate of food in front of her. It was time both of them got out of their comfort zones.

She raised her glass. "We never toasted."

"You are right, we didn't. You want to do the honors?"

"I do." She grinned, looking him in the eye. "To new beginnings."

His eyes darkened. "To new beginnings."

As they clinked their glasses together, he winked at her.

Tonight was going to be an interesting night.

Chapter Fourteen

THEY MET GIBSON DOWNTOWN, and the trio walked down Jefferson Street, popping in and out of the businesses that had art on display. Their first stop had been the Acadiana Center for the Arts. The huge two-story building was lit up like a Hollywood awards show.

"Ooh! Free champagne!" Carly exclaimed. "I like this already."

They strolled through one of the bigger exhibits, a room full of big canvases of splotchy neon colors that reminded Joey of a 1960s tie dyed t-shirt.

"This looks like some of the art my uncle did back in the sixties," Gibson said. "He farmed 'shrooms and liked to trip on acid."

Joey laughed. "That's kinda what I was thinking!"

Carly punched him in the arm. "I don't know, it's kinda cool." She turned her head one way then the other. "I have no idea what it's supposed to represent. But, hey, the champagne is free."

After leaving the ACA, they made their way through various other bars and shops, stopping for a drink or to stroll through and look at the local artwork. One of Carly's favorite places had been the store with the brightly colored prints and paintings. She had walked out with a print by an artist out of New Orleans with a crawfish holding a bottle of beer in one hand and the world on a fork in the other like Triton. The caption beneath read "I wanna roux the world."

"This is too cool," she said pulling the piece of the bag to admire it again. "I have to do this again next month. Did you see the others? I can get a set. These will look cute in the kitchen. These reds and blues will really pop against the yellow walls."

Carly came to a complete stop on the sidewalk.

"What is it?" Joey asked.

"Next month. I just said next month."

"And?"

"I guess it just hit me that I will still be here next month. I hadn't really stopped and thought about it."

"I suppose that's a good thing. You seem to have a plan."

She nodded, tucking her hand into his arm. "You know? I think you're right. Let's go find Emily and Noah. They're waiting for us at Legends."

• • • •

LILY HAD A BEER READY for Carly as she walked up to the bar. "And for your friend?"

"I'll have the same," Joey said.

Carly joined Emily and Noah at a small table in the corner while Joey waited on the drinks.

"I love this," Carly said. There's so much to see. They even had a little play going on at one of the theatres. We had the Gibson grand tour. He took us to all the spots."

"Oh, yeah?" Emily asked. "That's awesome. We've been sitting here watching the foot traffic. I'm trying to see how many people I might expect if I decide to open next month."

"There were quite a few people I saw. And I took some pictures of the set-ups people had with wine and whatnot. Some had sandwich trays, others had fruits and cheese, some had just wine. Are you thinking of doing something like that?"

"Yes. I just need to find some artists and musicians."

"I'm just the person to find you some musicians. I'm so excited about this! You know that means now I have to go out and listen to some to see who would be a good fit."

Emily rolled her eyes. "That sounds like such a chore for you."

Carly raised the bottle and rolled it across her forehead as if wiping sweat away. "Oh, yeah. It's tough."

"I will definitely leave all that up to you. And any drinks specials you think would work."

"I'll get to work on that. I'm sure I can find some cool stuff on Pinterest. Maybe we could do themes?"

"That sounds awesome. Just keep me updated. Now, how about we meander down the street and leave these two to the LSU game? We're going to stop by Bite Me. Gemma wants to come."

"Girl's night!" Carly said.

Emily laughed. "For a little while, at least." She kissed Noah goodbye, while Carly gave Joey an awkward hug. It seemed weird leaving him there on a date night, but she knew he was much happier sitting there than tagging along with her looking at more art.

As they stepped out onto the sidewalk, Emily turned to Carly. "So, how's it going?"

"It's kinda weird."

"That's pretty much any first date, isn't it?"

"True. I guess they all have different degrees and kinds of weirdness. I can't say it was the weirdest date I've ever been on. There was that guy who wanted to bring his mom that one time. Or the guy who invited me to take a cross country trip after our first date. Or I—"

"Okay, okay!" Emily laughed. "Let's not focus on those. You know Joey. That's the only thing that makes it weird. It's just something different. Relax."

"You're so right." Carly exhaled a deep breath. "Let's go see what's going on. We have an Art Walk event to plan for next month."

• • • •

"SOOOO, HOW IS IT GOING?" Noah asked as the women walked away.

"You know this is kinda weird, right?"

"What?"

"Me going out on a date. With Carly. Your sister."

"Oh, come on. What are we, twelve? You two are grown."

"It's been fun so far. A little awkward, but fun."

"That's good. What's next?" Noah asked.

"I don't know yet. I guess we will see."

"You still okay with heading out earlier tomorrow?"

"Yeah. And I guess I need to plant to look at apartments soon. I may text Ryder. I know he stayed with Grace when she lived in New Orleans. He might be familiar with something."

"Good idea. I'll ride with you when you decide to go."

He set the bottle down on the bar and spun it around a few times in his palms. "I asked Carly if she wanted to come."

Noah exhaled. "To look for places with you or to live?"

"To live."

"I don't think that's a good idea." It was Noah's turn to fidget. He pulled at the damp label on his bottle. "What would she do there? Bartend again? We both know that's not what she needs to do. If that's what she wants to do, that's fine. But I don't think she will. She looks happy here. Happier than I've seen her in a while."

"Yeah, you're right. I just thought about her in the Quarter, writing her stories."

"She can visit. Besides, wasn't she just telling us about that writer she met here? That may do her more good than the Quarter. It may be exactly what she needs. Someone to point her in the right direction."

"True. It's just going to be weird. We've been roommates for a couple of years now."

"And now you aren't. Don't make things more complicated than they are."

Joey laughed. "You got that right."

"Now, what do you think of this new coach LSU has? They call him Coach O?"

"If he keeps winning like this, I definitely think he's a keeper."

• • • •

BACK AT THE APARTMENT, Carly posed the piece of art she had bought earlier. "How do you think that looks?"

"It looks great," Joey responded, halfway looking at it.

"You aren't even really looking at it."

"It looks fine, Carly. It needs a frame, though."

"Of course it does. I'll go to the store sometime this weekend and pick something up." She rested the print against the wall and turned to Joey. "Gemma told me they have karaoke at a Mexican restaurant here in town. They go a lot. Says the guy is really good. I'm going to go check it out one night with them."

"That's great. It should be fun. Margaritas and music are always a good combo. Are you going to sing?"

Carly blushed. "I don't know. This is Lafayette, not Bon Chance. It's easier to make a fool out of yourself in a small town."

"Umm, Cat's Meow?" He referenced the popular karaoke bar on Bourbon Street.

"That's New Orleans. It's like they expect you to make a fool out of yourself."

Joey grabbed a couple of beers out of the fridge and popped the lids off. He handed one to Carly. "It sounds like you're settling in well here."

"I think so. Everyone is so friendly. It's like a bigger Bon Chance."

"That's great." He looked down. "When do you think you'll come back home? To visit?"

"I don't know. I need to. I need to grab some more stuff. But I just don't know if I'm ready yet."

"It's okay. I understand. I miss you, though. The house is too quiet without you."

She stepped into his embrace. "I miss you too. I'm really glad you came up here this weekend. And I'm really glad we had tonight."

He stepped back for a moment and lifted her chin gently, "Had? I don't think we're quite finished yet."

His eyes darkened, and Carly's knees went weak. His other hand snaked around her waist and pulled her against his body so close she was sure he would be able to feel her heart pounding.

Slowly, he lowered his head to hers. So slowly, she swore time stopped for a moment. When his lips touched hers, she lost all train of thought.

The kiss was soft and slow at first, an exploration. This time there was no reason to rush off, no pouring down rain, no hurricane to run from. It was just the two of them and the storm that was swirling between them.

Chapter Fifteen

My friend Morgan asked me to go with him to his company Christmas party, so I go along. And of course, afterward, we go to the Wahoo. It's Friday but not too crowded. It's like that during the holidays. People are getting together for company parties and other family celebrations. We say hello to everyone. Morgan goes to play pool, and I order a drink. I excuse myself to go to the ladies' room. I get back to the bar and notice the bartender hasn't brought my drink. There's only like five people in the bar, and I'm drinking beer, nothing to mix, shake, or pour. Where is my drink? And where is the bartender?

I start looking around the bar, and finally see her. She's crying. I go around the bar to see what's going on. Her boyfriend has broken up with her. No one likes a bawling bartender, so I grab my own beer and go to my seat and try to console her. I do everything, including getting up to serving drinks for the other patrons. It's no use. Every time I get her calm, she starts sobbing again. I send her home and take over her shift.

While I've been consoling the bartender and serving the others, another man I've talked to in the Wahoo has come in. His name is Jameson. He is another hottie. He's got the Cajun complexion. He's tall, tanned a mocha color, and oh so handsome. He's a contractor, so he's got great arms from swinging hammers and hauling stuff around all day.

I've left my phone and keys on the other side of the bar while I work. Jameson is still playing pool, so he hasn't been watching them, and Jameson has picked up my phone. I see him with it.

"What are you doing?" I ask.

"I'm trying to program my number into your phone, but I can't get it to work."

He can't get it to work because I dropped my phone in a beer recently and now some of the functions don't work.

I grab my phone and go about my business. Later, my phone rings. It's Jameson. He's programmed his number into my phone. I see it ring, and I glance at him. I look down at the phone but don't answer. Instead, I turn to chat with another customer.

I hear him laugh, and it makes me smile. The phone signals a voicemail, and I listen to it. It's Jameson's deep voice.

"It's Jameson. I'm standing here across the bar looking at you."

Okay, stalker.

"I don't know if you're dating anyone. I'm not, but I'd really like to take you to dinner. I'm not going to stalk you."

Woo-hoo!

"And I'm not calling you back. If you're interested, call me."

Damnit. Isn't that an intriguing message?

I'm wound up when I get off work, so I give him a call. We talk for a bit, and I ask if he wants to go grab breakfast at the diner. He says he's not going back out. he's at home in his pajamas. He invites me over. I laugh. I tell him of course not. I know what men want when they invite a woman over at two a.m. He says it's not about that. He just wants to hang out and laugh. I still refuse.

I finally give in but don't go without establishing ground rules. If he tries anything, I will beat him with my boot. We do end up hanging out, laughing, and having a good time. No mocha cheesecake for me, though. As I leave, I tell him to call me for dinner. He says he will when he has a babysitter. Jameson is a single dad and has custody of his boy. We'll see. I don't believe men when they tell me that. Not about the babysitter part, but about the calling.

Another interesting prospect. But is he Prince Charming?

• • • •

CARLY TOSSED THE BLANKETS aside. She was giving up on sleep after rolling over and over like a rotisserie chicken all night long. The sun was barely peeking through the curtains as she got up quietly. She was careful not to wake Joey, who still slept on the couch in the living room.

"Let's take this slow and enjoy it," he had said after ending the kiss that had literally curled Carly's toes.

Enjoy, she did—so much so that the memory of that kiss burned through her mind all night.

The apartment was so small that if she started coffee, it would disturb, so she decided against it. She opted instead for a bottle of water from the fridge.

Stepping back into the living room, she saw he had woken up. He lay there, his hair all messy, Sammy tucked by his side.

"Good morning," he said, smiling.

"Morning. I didn't mean to wake you."

"It's all good. I think Noah wanted to head out early this morning, anyway. He's meeting me at the home improvement store. We need a few things for repairs in town."

"Oh, okay. Want me to make some coffee?"

"Sure."

He got up from the sofa and stretched. Carly resisted the urge to stare at his shirtless chest and the muscles in his arms. The arms that had wrapped around her last night.

Arms that made her feel safe, and oh so sexy.

He crossed the room and hugged her close for a moment then kissed the top of her head. She smiled and rested her head on his shoulder.

He felt like home. Always had.

"Let me get a shower. Want to have coffee on the porch? I can go for breakfast in a bit."

She nodded as he slowly stepped back.

Carly hummed as she measured out the coffee for the machine. When done, she stepped outside to let Sammy go do her business. Carly sat on the top step while she watched the little dog sniff around, detecting the night animals that had trailed through.

A soft breeze blew through, and Carly shivered. Winter was just around the corner. That meant Thanksgiving, the holidays, and another New Year were too. How different the holidays would be this year. No Halloween party at Snapper's. What about Thanksgiving? Would Ruby return from Austin to host dinner at the Redbird? Would anything be the same?

She heard Joey come through the door. He leaned down with a steaming mug of coffee. He scooted in beside her on the step. "It was finished, so I made you a cup.

"Thank you."

"What are you thinking about?" he asked.

"The holidays are coming up."

"Yeah."

"It's going to be weird."

"Just different, Carly. Not everything new is weird."

She laughed. "Not to you, maybe."

"Just take it one day at a time. Breathe."

She exhaled a deep breath. "You're right. I can't worry about that. Tomorrow, I go back to work at the café. I'm going to eventually meet with Dawn about my work. I can't wait for you to meet her, Joey. After that, who knows?"

"I want to see you again soon. Is that okay with you?"

"Yes, I'd like that. I'm sure we can find something to do."

He threw his arm around her shoulder and hugged her close. "Yes, we will."

He stood and held a hand down for her. "Come on. Let's have another cup of coffee and some breakfast before I have to head back to Bon Chance."

"Breakfast? Now you're talking. There's this great place for beignets. Not as good as New Orleans, of course, but you know..."

He opened the door for her. "If you sweet talk me, I'm quite sure I can arrange for some New Orleans beignets next time I come in."

"You know how to spoil a woman, you know that?"

"Not any woman, Carly. Just you."

Her heart skipped a little beat at the gentleness of his voice. This was new. Different. And very, very nice.

• • • •

AFTER MORE COFFEE AND even more kisses, it was time for him to go. "See you soon?" Joey asked.

"Yep."

"I can't wait." He patted Sammy on the head before pulling Carly close for a kiss. His lips moved slowly against hers, teasingly. She wanted to beg him to stay just a little while longer.

To lose herself in these feelings. As he slowly pulled away, she stifled a frustrated groan.

He flashed her a dimpled grin, grabbed his travel bag, and was gone.

She watched him through the door as he drove away. She knew what she was going to do with the rest of her day. She was going to make a cheesecake. It may not be the particular cheesecake she wanted five minutes ago, but it was what she was going to get. For now, anyway.

"That's about right, make my own cheesecake," she muttered. "That's a whole other journal entry."

She went in the kitchen, made a mimosa, then put her hair in a ponytail. It was time to get down to business.

Carly grabbed the box from the cabinet and turned it around to read the directions.

"All right, three steps. Well, two, really. I bought a premade crust." She read through the directions again. "How hard can this be? I'm making cheesecake from a box."

She dumped the contents of the box onto the counter. Three plastic bags slid out.

She skimmed the directions. "Beat? You mean I have to use a beater? Damnit. Let me see if there's one in here."

Quickly, she rummaged through the small kitchen. Not a single beater in sight. "Oh, well, full speed ahead. We'll figure this out."

She dumped the bag of cream-colored powder into the white mixing bowl, then carefully measured the amount of milk necessary.

"Beat until thick," she said as she began to stir.

She mixed the cheesecake until her right hand began to cramp. She switched the spoon to the other hand. "Man, this must be what it's like making a roux from scratch. If I do this again, I'm buying a mixer."

Finally, she held the spoon up with some of the mixture on it and watch it slowly drip down. "That looks good enough to me."

As if she was painting a piece of art like ones at Art Walk, she spooned the cheesecake onto the waiting crust. She made swirls, smoothed them out, then swirls again.

When she was finished, she stood back and grinned.

She popped the spoon in her mouth and licked the rest of the cheesecake. She scooped a bit from the bowl and leaned down to let Sammy have a taste. When the dog tapped her tail on the floor, Carly took that as a good sign.

"I, Carly, have officially made my first cheesecake."

She grabbed her phone and took a picture. If ever a picture qualified as "food porn," this was it.

Chapter Sixteen

NOVEMBER 25TH

"Well, pretty lady," Daniel says. "Speaking of Christmas, what is it you want Santa to bring you?"

"I don't know. I haven't really thought about that. But you know what? I think it would be nice to have a boyfriend for Christmas this year. I've been single a while. And it would be nice to do all the usual holiday things with someone. I'm tired of decorating the tree by myself."

"You, Carly? Tell us again how that last date of yours went," John says.

My dating disasters are popular afternoon discussions. After the last one, I declared "men-opause" for what might be the tenth time in my life. I'm too young for real menopause, but that's what I call it when I'm taking a pause from all men and dating.

"Carly, with your luck, you should have started looking months ago," Daniel says.

"Is that right?" I ask after hitting him with the bar towel I keep tucked in my back pocket.

"Yes."

"I think that's a challenge. I think that's what I'm going to do. I'm going to find me a good man by Christmas."

"Look, you have two right here," says John.

"That's not what I mean."

"This is going to be interesting," Daniel says.

"You'd better keep a notebook handy. No telling what kind of writing you can get out of this."

"Oooh! Great idea!" I exclaim. "I can keep a journal and record how my search is going." Recently, I had pulled out my writer's pen and started playing around with story ideas. This was a great one. All I want for Christmas is a real good man. I smile, pondering the possibilities. I could even start a blog! Since Daniel is a retired journalist, I often give him pieces of my writing to critique. He wields a mean red pen. "Daniel, you are awesome! Dust off that pen. We're going to do some writing."

· · · ·

"THIS IS IT, SAMMY. The moment of truth," Carly said as she slid her spoon into the cheesecake. She raised the dessert to her nose and sniffed it before tasting it, as if it might have spoiled or ruined in the hour it had sat in the fridge. "Smells good. Like it should." She closed her eyes and slid it into her mouth.

Perfection. The strawberries were tart, but sweet. The cheesecake itself was creamy.

Carly's eyes went wide. "I did it! I made a cheesecake! All by myself!"

She took another bite, savoring the moment.

"This calls for a celebration. But where?" She snapped her fingers "Turtles." The little bar Lucky had taken her to after their fishing trip. That was exactly what she needed. Some sun, water, and cold beer. She finished the cake off in a couple more bites, grabbed her journal, and was on the road.

· · · ·

LUCKY GROANED AND OPENED one eye, "Oh, man." He knew it had been a bad idea to go meet Ryder and Julien at the Broken Spoke. It never turned out well. The three always wanted to out-flirt, out-dance, and out-drink the other ones. His head hurt, he was sore, and he had numbers in his phone he had no intention of calling.

He climbed out of bed and pulled his pants on. Feeling something in his pocket, he reached back and found a soft piece of fabric. He pulled it out and groaned. How had he gotten pretty pink panties in his pocket?

"Ryder, you ass," he muttered, his voice hoarse. He grabbed his phone and headed to the kitchen. He needed coffee. And aspirin. Cooking at Turtles later today would be rough.

He shook a couple of pain relievers out of the bottle and chased it with a sip of coffee, still cursing Ryder. Thank goodness he only came to town once or twice a year.

He threw a couple of pieces of bread in the toaster to snack on before heading to the shower.

• • • •

HE HAD SEEN CARLY'S car in the lot when he drove up. As he walked in the bar, he raised his sunglasses so he could look for her. When he didn't see her, he pulled out his phone to text.

He walked up to the bar and greeted the bartender and owner, who had a beer ready for him. "Some tomato juice too, please, Jessie. I need a hangover cure."

"You? A hangover?"

"It was all Ryder's fault."

"Ryder? Where's that scoundrel been?"

"He was in town this weekend."

"Next time you see him, tell him to come by and see me."

"I definitely will." He leaned in and kissed Jessie on the cheek. "Now, I'm going to get a bit of fresh air before I fire up the pit."

"If that doesn't wake you up, that cute little blonde will."

"Blonde?"

"Yeah, she came in a bit ago. She's been out there with a book."

"Hmmm, this, I need to see."

She placed two beers and a small Styrofoam cup of tomato juice on the bar. "Here's one for her too. On the house. For putting up with you."

He laughed and winked before heading out the back door. "You love me. You know it."

He was still chuckling when he spotted Carly sitting on a stool that faced the water. When she heard him, she turned and smiled, and he felt a little catch in his heart.

"What's up, *cher*?" he asked, handing her the fresh beer.

"Just enjoying some sunshine. Watching the water. That dog." She pointed to a black retriever that was playing in the shallow water of the boat launch.

"Oh, that's Rio. He's Jessie's dog. He hangs out here while she's working. In a little bit, I'll light the pit for Sunday barbeque for the game, and he'll be all up here begging for a treat here and there."

"Barbeque? That sounds great. I might have to stick around."

"You should, it's usually a pretty good spread. It's kind of like a potluck. See all these little houses around here? They come hang out to watch the game. I volunteered to cook today. But sometimes I'll go to Whiskey River too."

"Whiskey River?"

"A place just down the road a ways. They have dancing every Sunday. I'll have to bring you one day." He gestured down at his tennis shoes. "I'll need to wear my boots. And maybe we can get Ryder to come as well. He has a good time too."

"That would be awesome."

"I'll talk to him. With you here now, he's more likely to come. He sure cares about you."

"And I love him."

Lucky raised an eyebrow, and Carly laughed.

"No, not like that. We'd kill each other. I made my peace with that some time ago. We are much better friends."

"You can never have too many of those," he said.

"I agree." She held out her beer to toast. "To friends."

"To *new* friends," he said.

She smiled. "I'll drink to that."

He motioned to her journal that was laying on the table. "Trying to get some writing done?"

"Yeah, jotting a few things down. Nothing is sticking yet."

He pointed his bottle out toward the water. "If this view doesn't inspire you, I don't know what will. Now, I think I'll have one more, and it will be time for me to start the barbeque."

"Sounds good to me. I'll just have a seat and enjoy this gorgeous day."

"You do that, *cher*." He nodded and stood. "I'll be back."

"Good deal. I'll be here. You said the magic word."

He laughed. "Food? Girl, we're going to have to teach you how to cook. It's easier than dancing. You got this."

"I may hold you to that."

"*Cher*, you can hold me to anything you like." He winked and turned to go back into the bar.

• • • •

CARLY MADE HER LAST selection on the jukebox. Not being a regular, she had made her choices mostly from the "Most Played" list, which consisted mostly of older rock, country, and swamp pop. There was no Aaron Lewis, but she was okay with that. Maybe it was okay that her playlist changed as her life did. She'd played a few old bar favorites and added in some Kenny Chesney to top it off.

As she ordered another beer, and the smell of burning coals wafted in through the open door. The music, the conversation, the smell of the water mixed with the scent of charcoal was just like Snapper's on a Sunday. Pain sliced through her, and she reached out to the jukebox for support.

The picture Joey sent of the bar's destruction flashed through her mind. Broken windows, sagging pink insulation, pieces of what used to be the roof on the ground.

She inhaled a deep breath, pushing the pain away. The urge to order a shot, to drink until she forgot was strong, but she had to drive home. She could mourn tomorrow.

She went back out onto the deck. The barroom had become suddenly way too small.

• • • •

LUCKY CHECKED ON THE coals that were flaming up nicely. He opened the back door and started to the bar, but a movement in the corner caught his eye. It was Carly, her hand gripping the jukebox. He watched as she struggled to breathe.

"Shit," he muttered. Should he go over to her? He didn't know her that well. This had awkward written all over it. He kept an eye on her and continued to the bar. He pulled out his phone and typed out a quick text.

Lucky: Your girl isn't doing well today.

He ordered a beer and kept his eye on the phone. He was only a couple of sips in when he got a reply.

Ryder: Where is she?

Lucky: Turtles.

Ryder: Oh, shit.

Lucky watched as Carly went back outside onto the deck. He was about to go check on his fire again when his phone rang. It was Ryder.

"What's up?" he said as he answered.

"That's the one place that would remind her of Snapper's. It's the last place she needs to be right now. Damnit. I'll text her. Maybe she'll head back to Lafayette. If not, call me back and let me know."

Lucky thought for a moment before responding. As far as he could see, Carly was a grown woman and could make her own decisions. "All right."

"Thank you, cousin."

Lucky hung up without responding. This whole thing was beginning to leave a bad taste in his mouth. He took another sip of his beer and went out to join Carly on the deck.

• • • •

CARLY STARED OUT AT the water, so lost in her thoughts she jumped when Lucky set his beer down on the table.

"Sorry," he said. "Didn't mean to startle you. I don't usually scare women."

Carly laughed. "I was a thousand miles away. Well, more like about two hundred miles away."

"Thinking about home?"

"Something like that."

"You know what helps get your mind off your troubles?" His eyes lit up.

"I'm sure I can guess with you."

"I was going to say," he bit his full bottom lip suggestively, "cooking."

Carly shook her head. "Oh, no. Cooking can be the root of my troubles."

"Oh, come on, now." He reached out for her hand. "Come see."

Carly took his hand, and he led her to the grill.

"You must want the fire department to come out here if you want me to cook."

He laughed. "Oh, ye of little faith. You are going to cook these hamburgers. I am going to drink my beer, supervise, and continue to recuperate from your friend trying to kill me last night. You are going to do a good deed for a struggling friend."

"By cooking?"

"Yep. Watch." He held his hand over the coals. "Test the heat by holding your hand above the coals. When it feels like it's hot enough to cook, but not too hot to burn, it's time to put the burgers on." He motioned to the pile of patties Jessie had brought out and put on the table beside the grill. "Season them with a little salt, pepper, and Tony's on both sides. Then put them on. If it sizzles, it's perfect."

Carly set about following his directions and started seasoning the burgers while Lucky watched. When they were proper-
ly salted and peppered, she put them on and was excited to hear
that little sizzle.

"There you go."

He continued to instruct Carly on proper burger grilling,
telling her when to flip, when to add the slices of cheese, and
when to pull them off the heat. As they finished, Lucky took
the trays into the bar for the patrons to begin making plates.
She found a rhythm, and before she knew it, she was down to
the last few patties. She finished them up and put them on the
tray.

"Look how easy that was! And you didn't burn one of
them."

"No, and the fire department didn't come. I consider that a
win."

"You going to come have a burger? Taste how you did?"

She nodded. "Give me a minute."

"Got it." He reached out and placed his hand on her shoulder. "You don't give yourself enough credit, Carly. I think it's
time you started realizing that."

"I think you're right. I think it's time I realized a lot of
things."

He squeezed her shoulder lightly. "Come on in when
you're ready. I'll buy you a beer."

"Food and free beer? Another win!"

He laughed and walked away, leaving Carly alone.

She put her feet up in the chair across from her and leaned
back, gazing over at the grill. She had done it. She had made

probably twenty-five or thirty hamburger patties for today's meal, not one overcooked or underdone.

Cheesecake *and* hamburgers all in one day. She was starting to think this cooking thing may be something she could actually do. Maybe not on an Emily, Glinda, or Joey scale, but hey, if it was good enough for a bar full of hungry customers, it was good enough for her.

She took a last sip. Lucky owed her a drink, and she was going to collect.

• • • •

LUCKY SAT WITH A SMALL group of regulars gathered at a table in the middle of the room. A football game was on, but it wasn't the Saints, so they watched it half-heartedly. It was a routine he knew well. If the Saints weren't on, he'd still stop in on most Sundays for a cold beer and some conversation.

He usually spent the weekends at the camp, away from the hustle and bustle of Lafayette, not that it was a big city or anything. He just preferred the quiet. He was a "take his coffee out onto the deck and watch the sunrise over the swamp" kind of person. It suited him.

Every now and then, he would get the *envie,* and wonder what it would be like to share that with a woman. To see her standing there in one of his t-shirts, mug in hand, hair messy. A vision of Carly flashed through his mind, and his body stiffened. He knew exactly what he would do. Take that mug, set it on the railing, and lose himself in her kiss.

"Lucky?" His friend, Paul, poked him. "What ya thinkin' about over there? We're talking about this monster catfish Jerry caught the other day, and you didn't even bat an eye."

Lucky smiled. "Nothing much, really. Just about some stuff I should do one morning."

"Looks to me like you're thinking about a different kind of fishin,'" Jerry said, slapping him on the shoulder.

Lucky adjusted the ball cap he wore. "Oh, now, you know I never tell."

"I know, damn the bad luck. Us old married guys like to live victoriously through you."

Paul laughed, nearly spewing beer on the table. "You damned old idiot, you mean vicariously."

"I don't know about you, but I feel victorious every time I get a little you know what." He raised both eyebrows and giggled.

"I can't even deal with you two today. I'm gonna go get another one. Y'all need anything?"

"Nah, we're good. We'll wait for Jessie to come. She's a lot cuter walking away than you are."

Lucky rolled his eyes and made his way to the bar where Jessie was waiting.

"Make that two. He owes me one," he heard Carly say, walking up behind him.

"Add another one. I do owe her one. She cooked all those burgers today."

"Don't tell me you let him con you into doing all the work today just because he has a hangover," Jessie scolded.

Carly smiled. "No, I really did enjoy it. It got my mind off a few things."

"Well, good. The burgers were excellent too. We may just have to have you out here some more."

"I would like that. This place reminds me of home."

"And that's what it is, *cher,*" Jessie said. "It's our home. See those old guys at that table? They both own houseboats that are docked a little ways behind us. They come in here every day to gossip and talk shit."

"And they are very good at both," Lucky said. "Great guys, though. Would do anything in the world for you."

"Sounds like my kind of people."

"Come back any time." Jessie winked before leaving to check on another customer who had walked in.

"Hey, Lucky," the guy who had just come in said. "You still entering that cook-off in Abbeville?"

"You bet. I compete, and win, every year."

"We'll see about that this year. I've been working on my recipe."

"We'll just see about that." Lucky laughed.

"Good to see you, Lucky."

"Same here, Steve. This is Carly," Lucky said, gesturing over.

"Hmmmm, Lucky never brings his women here. You must be special."

Carly laughed. "It's not like that. I just came out here for a drink or two today and to enjoy the scenery."

"It's a good place. I gotta head out. See you soon, and nice to meet you, ma'am."

"Cook-off?" Carly asked as he walked away. "I love those. I never participate, of course, but it always feels good to do something for charity."

"Yeah, a vet clinic in Abbeville does one every year to benefit rescue dogs. Hank was a rescue, so I cook every year."

"Oh! I have to check that one out. When is it?"

"In a couple of weekends. You should come cook with me. I haven't lined up anyone to help yet, and it's an awful lot of work for just one person."

"Me, really?"

"Yes, you. You can come over a couple of times before the cook-off, and we can practice. What we don't eat, we'll bring to friends or here to Turtles."

"Hmmmm. I think I'd like that."

He reached out and tapped his bottle with hers. "Then, welcome to Team Get Lucky."

"That's your team name?"

"Yes." He grinned.

"We really have to work on that too. You teach me how to make gumbo, and I'll come up with a team name. 'Get Lucky,'" she repeated with an eyeroll.

"You're the writer, not me."

"Wannabe writer."

He tapped the journal on the bar in front of her. "If you put actual words on paper and make sentences and stories, you, my friend, are a writer. Get used to it. Now, I'll text you sometime this week, and we'll make plans for you to come over. Bring your dog too."

"That sounds great. And now that you mention food, I think I'm going to go fix myself a burger before the game gets started."

She smiled at him, and he cursed as his heart did that flutter thing it wasn't supposed to do. But damnit, if this other guy was so into her, why hadn't he made a move yet? And more importantly, why did this guy seem to let her doubt herself so much?

He sipped his beer as she finished her burger and sat down beside him. She took one bite, and her eyes went wide.

"This is delicious."

"I told you. Now, just you wait. We are going to bring home that cook-off trophy."

Chapter Seventeen

CARLY PULLED UP IN front of the cabin and took a deep breath. "C'mon, Sammy."

The weenie dog jumped out and ran up the stairs to meet her newest friend, Duke, who was waiting for her, along with Lucky.

"You didn't chicken out," he said with a smile.

She stiffened. "Carly Devereaux never chickens out from a challenge."

He laughed. "Come on in. I have everything ready out back. If you burn something, you won't stink up my house."

"I'm not burning anything. You'll see," she said with more bravado than she felt. She could do this. She would do this. It was high time she learned how to cook something real.

She followed Lucky through the house and out onto the back patio. He already had a few things assembled, and the radio was playing.

"First things first." He handed her a beer. "This is a necessity."

"Is that right?"

"Yep, my grandma's secret recipe."

She shook her head then went to wash her hands. When she was finished, she said, "What do we do first?"

"I'm going to go grab the meat. I'm not teaching you how to make a roux today. I'm teaching you the easiest way. When you get more comfortable, you'll start to experiment on your own, if you want, or just keep doing what you're doing. It's up to you. That's the beauty of gumbo. There's only one real rule."

"What's that?"

"Do not, under any circumstances, ever add tomatoes."

"Even I know that."

"Good deal." He went in the house to grab whatever else would be needed. The day was cold, and she was glad she'd worn a hooded jacket. When the burners got started, the heat would be welcome.

Lucky came back outside with several packages that he laid on the counter beside the burners. "Come see."

Lucky washed his hands and wiped them on a University of Lafayette hand towel he had near the sink, and handed her a knife. He gestured to the large wooden cutting board. "First, we're going to brown the meat."

He pushed packages of chicken and sausage toward her. "You start cutting up the chicken, and I'll start the pot."

He poured some oil into the weathered gray Magnalite and turned on the propane burner. That chore complete, he leaned against the railing and grabbed a beer.

"If we time this just right, we can get all the work done then sit back and watch the game. LSU plays 'Bama tonight, and we don't want to miss any of it."

Carly sliced the chicken into big chunks. Lucky took the cutting board and slid the meat into the waiting oil. It sizzled as it hit the pot. "Hear that? That's perfect. Now, we just add some seasoning." He reached for a container of Cajun seasoning. "Look, I don't measure. No one I know does, but this is how it should look." He shook the spices onto the chicken until it was evenly covered.

Carly nodded. Everything was easy so far. Not too stressful.

"Now, you just sit back and stir. Don't stir too much. Let it sit and cook. The more stuff that sticks to the bottom, the better the gumbo will be."

Carly leaned back and relaxed.

"There, you see? That's another of my grandma's secrets. You can't let the stress get to you. You gotta enjoy the process."

"Your grandmother seems like quite the woman."

"She is. She just celebrated her ninetieth birthday. When asked what the secret to living long is, she said, good food, good family, and good love," he said with a wink.

Carly exhaled a breath and picked up the wooden spoon. She was half tempted to hit him with it but was afraid that would only encourage him. Instead, she peered over the rim of the pot to check the progress. Everything seemed to be cooking along quite well, so she turned—right into Lucky. Instinctively, she put her hands out to steady herself, only to feel the rock-hard expanse of his chest. Feeling as if she'd been burned, she jerked her hands back.

His blue eyes clouded, and he was quiet for a moment before he said, "I just wanted to check on things."

Carly turned back to the pot. "I think everything is good here."

He exhaled. "It certainly looks that way."

• • • •

LUCKY TOOK A STEP BACK to get himself in check. If Ryder wasn't his cousin, he would have reached out and pulled Carly just a little closer and had a taste of those lips of hers. She had feelings for this Joey guy, he could tell. And damn it if that challenge didn't make her more appealing. He was a masochist, that was for sure. He should be out tonight at some sports bar with the game on looking for a woman who was looking for the same thing he was. A night of fun with no strings.

Carly? Carly came with all kinds of strings, and knots, and bows. Things that made life complicated. He looked over at the blonde beauty, stirring the pot with such concentration, and his stomach flip-flopped.

Doing the only thing he knew to do; he grabbed his phone and sent a text to one of the women whose numbers he had found on his phone after his night out with Ryder. He needed the distraction.

• • • •

ABOUT AN HOUR LATER, Carly stirred the brown liquid simmering in the pot. She reached for her phone and took a picture, which she sent to Joey.

Carly: I'm making gumbo! Like, real gumbo!

There was no immediate answer, so she took a seat in one of the chairs on the porch. Lucky had been quiet since their run-in by the stove. He'd given her directions and supervised her progress, but for the most part had kept his distance. She was glad for that. Carly knew she was attracted to Lucky, but didn't know what she should do about it, if anything. It seemed like the same old story all over again. She was attracted to the wrong person at the wrong time. And she was still thinking of Joey. It was Joey's texts she wanted before she went to bed, and the first ones she wanted to see when she woke up. But he was packing to move to New Orleans. And she was in Lafayette and staying there for the time being.

Carly looked out at the bayou, at the brown water passing slowly by. New Orleans. Her favorite city in the world, and her best friend was moving there. If she said the word, she could go with him. He wouldn't say no.

What would she do, though? Go from managing a bar to bartending again? Take a step back? She was happy here. She couldn't do it. Not even for Joey.

Chapter Eighteen

CARLY CLUTCHED THE black-clipped manuscript close to her chest. In a few moments, she would be handing her writing off to Dawn. The butterflies in her stomach were not the good kind.

She had made plans to see Joey the next morning and had decided to give the book to her before leaving. The plan was to meet at Legends after her shift at the café. After she opened the door, she exhaled a nervous breath as she looked for Dawn.

She spotted her quickly, seated at the corner of the bar with Dylan.

"First, a drink," she said to herself, stepping up to the bar. She placed her order before flipping through the manuscript. Two hundred pages of her writing were about the in the hands of a published author. What if it was crap?

The bartender returned with her drink, and she took a big gulp, hoping for some liquid courage.

"It's now or never," she said, squaring her shoulders. The quick bass of the rock song playing from the band mimicked the beating of her heart.

"Hi, Carly," Dylan said as she approached. "Pull up a seat."

"Is this your manuscript?" Dawn asked.

Carly could only nod, silently pushing the book toward Dawn, who laughed.

"You can relax. I promise I won't bite. I leave that to my characters."

Carly blew out a breath, finally relaxing. One way or another, she was going to know if what she had worked so hard on was actually worth anything.

Dawn put the book in her backpack that slung over the back of her bar stool, "I'll give it a look this weekend. I'm helping out at the festival Sunday, but I should still have time to give it a glance. You should come by, support a good cause."

"I might do that if I'm back in time."

"Oh?"

"I'm heading to Bon Chance tomorrow morning. I need to get some more of my things. I'm kind of living out of a suitcase right now."

"Oh, yeah, that can suck."

Dylan chimed in. "Oh, and you can always volunteer if you'd like. We're always looking for people to help sling beer."

"I can definitely do that. When I get back into town, I'll stop by. Where will you be? I've never been to this festival."

"Beer tent near the main stage. That's where we always are."

"Great. Sounds like fun." Carly did want to check this out. Everything she had heard about it sounded like a good time. She would have enough time Sunday after her return from Bon Chance.

The talk turned to discussing what bands would be playing when. Carly was excited to hear one of her favorites, Geno Delafosse, would be performing Sunday. She would definitely have to go. She was already looking forward to it. A great way to finish out what should be a great weekend. She would get to spend some time with Joey then come back and listen to some local music. Finally, she brushed her nervousness aside, relaxed, and just enjoyed the moment. Life was slowly but surely moving forward.

Chapter Nineteen

CARLY DROVE UP TO SNAPPER'S.

She stopped breathing.

Her hand flew up to her face.

Snapper's.

She couldn't breathe.

All the work. The memories. The cook-offs. Was nothing now.

She found a piece of rubble from the collapsed side big enough to sit on. She thought of all the memories she had there. Closing her eyes, she could see the bright tents outside as everyone prepped for the annual cook-off for Ben's scholarship fund. She could hear the karaoke sung by Grace and Gabe. She could even smell the hamburgers cooking for the busy lunch crowd.

Opening her eyes, she couldn't comprehend it. How could Snapper's just be in pieces?

Not only had she lost Ben, now she had lost Snapper's. The place she had dedicated to him. Where he had bought his bait before he'd gone fishing. Where they had hung out as kids buying root beer and candy cigarettes.

How could you lose someone twice?

Sobbing, she placed her face in her hands. Gulping sobs. Throat hurting sobs. Can't breathe sobs.

A hand touched her shoulder, and Joey said softly, "Come with me."

Wordlessly, she followed him, crawling into his Jeep, Sammy already on the floorboard.

She stared out the window, her vision blurred with tears.

They pulled up to the house they had shared until the hurricane.

Joey reached for her hand. "Whatever you need tonight, I am here for you."

Overwhelmed, she said, "I don't even know."

"Then, we will figure it out together. I'm going to cook, and you just do what you need to do. Scream, yell, cry, whatever. I'm here."

A tear fell, trailing down her cheek. Joey saw it and rubbed his thumb across it, and when she looked at him, she saw his own pain. The tears brimming in his soft brown eyes.

"You are not alone," he said. He pulled her close for a long hug. She wadded her hands in his shirt. She felt so empty. But not alone, and that comforted her. Sniffing, she took a step back.

Taking her by the hand, he led her to the sofa. After she sat, he grabbed a soft black and gold Saints throw and tucked it around her. Sammy immediately jumped up and burrowed under the blanket. Carly patted her head.

He handed her the remote. "Watch what you like, or put it on Pandora. I'm going to cook something."

"You're too good to me," Carly said, her voice shaky and hoarse.

"Not nearly. What if I decide to make smothered cabbage?"

Carly smiled in return. She absolutely hated the green vegetable and the way it stunk up the whole house. "Gross."

"Nah, it's not a cabbage kind of day. Let me see what I can whip up."

He crossed into the open kitchen and begin banging around the cabinet and refrigerator doors, humming along with the music Carly had decided to play. It wasn't long before the smell of onions, bell peppers, and garlic, the Cajun Trinity, filled the room.

Carly relaxed, letting her head hit the back of the sofa, closing her eyes. Exhausted emotionally and physically, she dozed off.

• • • •

RYDER: HOW IS SHE?

Joey stared down at the phone for a moment, wondering what to tell him. Carly wasn't okay. He hadn't seen her grieve like that since Ben died. He had known it would hit her hard when she saw Snapper's. Hell, it was hard on him. It took him weeks not to turn his head when he drove by. Not only was it their business, it had been a fixture in Bon Chance since forever. They used to sneak booze and cigarettes as teens and go sit on the dock and talk about their dreams. Joey raised an eyebrow. He had an idea for after dinner.

Joey: IDK

He sighed after responding to Ryder's text. It was the most honest answer he could give. She may not be okay now, but she would be. Carly was a fighter. She didn't see herself that way. But he did. Maybe he should tell her that more often.

He looked over and saw her sleeping. Her legs were curled up close to her, and even from where he was, he could see a tear escape and trickle down her cheek.

He needed to go to the store but didn't want to leave her. He grabbed his phone again to text Noah.

Joey: Can you do me a big favor? Carly is here, and I need to go to the store.

Noah: What do you need?

Joey sent him a list. He smiled when he got the response from Noah.

Noah: Boone's Farm? Really?

Joey: Trust me.

Noah: Oh, that's right up her alley. Be there in thirty.

Joey turned his attention back to the stove. Shrimp and sausage fettuccine coming up. It was one of her favorites. He had some fresh shrimp from a recent trip with Noah. Then with the garlic bread Noah would pick up, the meal would be perfect.

Preparations made, he leaned against the counter. He looked over at Carly. He had wanted her back home. But not this way. Not this sad.

He met Noah out on the porch, so as not to wake Carly or Sammy.

Noah said, "How is she?"

"It hit her hard, Noah. Really hard. It wasn't just a building to her. It was her safety net. Her sanctuary. We all know that."

"I know. Keep us posted. And let us know what else we can do. Emily is worried too."

Joey smiled. "I will. I'm going to take good care of her."

Noah reached out to clasp his hand. "I know you will, my brother."

He smacked him on the back. "See you tomorrow for the game?"

"Sure. It may be just what Carly needs to get her mind off all this."

Noah walked off, and Joey went back in the house quietly. He was surprised she was still sleeping. Usually, Sammy barked at any intrusion, but she seemed to sense her person needed rest.

He took the shopping bags Noah had brought and placed them on the counter. He put one bottle of Boone's in the freezer to cool quickly, and the other in the fridge. He grimaced, remembering the sweet taste and the hangovers they had always woken up with after a binge on Boone's.

Groceries put away, he checked on the food still cooking in the Magnalite and waited.

• • • •

SOUNDS IN THE KITCHEN woke Carly from her nap. She opened her eyes to see Joey padding around in the kitchen, just like always. The familiar sight comforted her, and she felt a little part of her heart heal, just a bit. She tugged the blanket aside and went to join him in.

"Well, hello," he said as she took a place at the bar. He went to the fridge and grabbed a beer. He opened it before sliding it in front of her.

"I need this," she said. "And about a hundred shots."

"I don't know about the shots, but I have something else." He lifted the lid to the pot so the aroma could drift out. "How about some fettuccine? It's ready. Let me make you a plate."

"That would be amazing. I'm starving."

After a few quick movements that told of his time in a service kitchen, he was setting a plate of pasta, salad, and a chunk of French bread in front of her.

She took a moment to breathe it all in. "Oh, my God, Joey, this smells amazing." Her eyes clouded over for a moment. "You definitely need to go to New Orleans."

He looked down at his own plate and pushed the food around, as if he didn't know what to say.

"It's okay, Joey." She reached out and placed her hand on his. "I get it."

He looked up and turned his hand so it was holding hers. "Thank you."

"I didn't at first," she blurted. "I was so mad. How could you? Just move on like that? But working at Cypress and getting to know a whole group of people, including real writers, has made me want to move on too." It was her turn to look down before continuing. "I just don't know what to move on to."

He leaned over the bar and placed a soft kiss on her head. "You'll figure it out, Carly. Just give it some time."

The words were reassuring, and she smiled. "You're so awesome, you know that?"

He blushed. "Oh, now. Finish that up. I have something in mind."

"I don't want to go anywhere."

"We're not, not really."

"Now I'm intrigued," she said and dug in.

Soon, Joey was collecting the plates and rinsing them for dishwasher.

"Put some shoes on and follow me," he said, grabbing a small ice chest and bag that was by the door.

Sammy jumped up, eager for an adventure. "Lead the way," Carly said with a nod.

She was surprised when they didn't jump in the Jeep but continued to trek down the road. Her heart constricted a little when she realized they were heading to Snapper's. Surely, he wouldn't be planning on hanging out on that empty lot.

He wasn't, she figured out as the skirted along the edge of the property and down toward the water where the docks were. She took in a breath of the familiar brackish air and heard the waves hit the wooden pier, and instantly she was reminded of high school. She turned to him and grinned. "You bringing me here to make out, Joey Delchamp?"

He reached out and placed his hands on her hips. "Hmmm, making out with Carly Devereaux under the moonlight? It's tempting. But that wasn't my plan then, and it's not my plan tonight. Have a seat, *cher*."

She sat on the dock, her legs dangling off the edge. She swung her feet back and forth and watched as the stars and moon reflected on the water.

"How many times did we sit here in high school?" she asked.

"Too many to count."

"True."

"Talking about all our hopes. Our dreams for the future. I was going to get out of this town."

"And you did. Houston and Biloxi."

"But I ended up back here. Stuck."

"And now you're not. Stuck. You can do anything you want to do, Carly. What do you dream about now?"

"Honestly, Joey, can't we just sit here? Just you and me and the sound of the waves?"

He wrapped his arm around her shoulder and pulled her close to him. She leaned into his warm embrace, enjoying the comfort he provided. He leaned down and kissed the top of her head. "Anything, Carly. Anything you want."

She exhaled a deep breath and scooted even closer. "Thank you, Joey. For everything."

They sat in silence, staring out into the darkness, hearing the water splashing softly. Carly's thoughts turned to the now destroyed Snapper's and her memories there. She looked up at the endless expanse of stars and wondered what, if anything, the universe was trying to tell her.

"You don't give yourself enough credit, Carly. I think it's time you started realizing that." Lucky's voice penetrated her thoughts. He was right.

"Joey?" she asked, mustering her strength for the words she was about to say.

"Yes?"

"I'm going back to Lafayette tomorrow."

"Tomorrow? I thought you were staying until Sunday?"

She reached for his hand. "Joey..." she exhaled, "I want to be by myself for a while."

"What do you mean?"

She bit her quivering bottom lip. "Alone. Completely alone. This is something I need to do." She emphasized the word "I."

"Oh." His voice was barely above a whisper.

"I've become too dependent on you, on this place. On everyone. I need to find out what I can do on my own. Find that Carly I used to be."

He chuckled. "I get it."

"You do?"

"I know something has been up with you for months now. If this is what you need, then I'm here for you. Even if I can't be *here* for you."

She laughed at his cheesy play on words.

"I love you. You know that."

"I know. And I love you." She heard the catch his is voice, and it tore her own heart to shreds. To leave him in the morning was going to be one of the hardest things she ever did.

He inhaled a deep breath. "New Carly, huh? I think this deserves a toast with this wonderful Strawberry Hill."

"You got it."

He poured them fresh glasses, the light pink liquid sparkling in the moonlight. "Here's to you, Carly. And to your new beginning."

Chapter Twenty

BACK IN LAFAYETTE, Carly wiped a tear away as she looked down at the picture frame in her hand. It was the last picture they had taken at Snapper's. And now, it was gone. She closed her eyes against the vision of the curtains flapping in the wind out of the broken window. The crumbled concrete, the broken glass glistening in the sun.

Watching Joey from her rearview mirror as she had driven away that morning. The tears she had seen in his eyes that mirrored her own.

Sammy thumped her tail on the wooden porch, and Carly leaned down to give her a reassuring pat on the head.

"It's okay, girl. We're just going to stay here a bit longer, that's all. Momma's got some stuff she needs to work out."

Saturday night. She should be getting ready for the busy night shift. She should be stocking, cleaning the bar, something.

She glanced down at her phone which had just signaled she'd received a text message.

Gemma: We're going to Tampicos for karaoke. Want to come?

Carly frowned. What was her alternative? Stay here and drown herself in her sorrows? Literally?

Carly: Sure. What time?

Gemma: Lucky will swing by in about an hour to pick you up.

Carly smiled. He had an uncanny ability to cheer her up.

Carly: I'll be ready.

Gemma: Great! Will see you then!

She finished off her beer and grabbed the frame from the table, stopping a moment to run her fingers along the glass. "C'mon, Sammy. Looks like I'm going out tonight. Nothing here but old ghosts."

• • • •

AN HOUR LATER ON THE dot, Lucky pulled into her driveway. Carly threw Sammy a treat from the bag on the counter. "Be good, girl. I'll be back."

She patted her back pocket to make sure she had her debit and ID cards and phone, and pushed the screen door open to go meet Lucky.

"You don't wait for a man to knock, do you, *cher*?" Lucky drawled as she started down the stairs.

"In my experience, if I waited for a man, I'd be skin and bones."

Lucky laughed. "You need some better men in your life."

Carly shook her head. "No, I have some pretty good ones. Just not ones I should date."

He opened the truck door for her, and she hopped in. The truck smelled like leather and cologne. Cajun music played from the radio.

He climbed in. "You ready? I hope you like Cajun music. My radio stays tuned to KBON."

"I love it. Just don't ask me to dance to it. Ryder has told me more than once that I'm hopeless."

"Maybe you just haven't had the right partner."

"Have you seen Ryder dance?"

"Yeah, but I also know his temperament. Maybe a more patient person would help."

"Yeah, no. So, you take photos, you dance, do you sing too?"

"Every now and then. I'm not great, but it works with the ladies." He looked over at her, and she saw his wink in the dashboard lights.

"You, my friend, should come with a warning label."

"Oh, and what would that be? 'Handle with care'?"

Carly laughed. "When I figure it out, I'll let you know."

• • • •

ABOUT TWENTY MINUTES later, they were walking through the doors of Tampicos. The eating area was off to the right, the bar to the left. Lucky placed a hand on her elbow and led her to the bar.

Gemma jumped off the bar stool and hugged Carly. "So glad you came! You're going to love it. I know it."

Her boyfriend and Lucky's brother, Jasper, was seated across the table. He nodded and tipped his cowboy hat in greeting.

"I'm sure I will. Let me order a drink real quick."

"I got that," Lucky said. "Beer?"

Carly nodded, and he went to the bar to order.

"I didn't know if you were going to come out, but I'm glad you did," Gemma said. "It must be rough, with everything going on."

Carly looked around the bar, wondering if she should have come at all. She wanted to forget Snapper's had been wiped out. Not reminded.

"I'm so sorry," Gemma said. "I didn't mean to...Oh, shit."

Lucky returned with two beers. "One for you, *cher*. It looks like you need it."

"That's my fault," Gemma said. "I promise to behave better for the rest of the evening. No depressing subjects."

"You're right about that. There will be no sad stuff around me. We're here to have a good time. Right?"

"Right!" Carly and Gemma said, the four of them tapping the tops of their bottles.

The waitress came around with menus, and the group was quiet while they perused the food options. Carly felt eyes on her and turned to see who might be looking at her.

A man was staring at her but looked away when Carly turned. He looked vaguely familiar.

"Something wrong?" Gemma asked.

"That guy, I think I know him from somewhere, and he keeps looking at me."

"Well, maybe he's been to Bon Chance? He may be a fisherman or something."

"Maybe so." Carly shrugged it off, turning her attention back to the menu.

The waitress returned to take their orders, and talk turned to the upcoming holiday, Halloween.

"Jasper and I are going to New Orleans for Halloween. They have the coolest parade. It's called the Krewe of Boo. The throw beads and Halloween stuff."

"That's exciting! I've always wanted to go to New Orleans for Halloween. I've done some of the ghost tours, but it would be fun to see it all decorated and creepy."

"You could come with us. We got a room at the Chateau Rouge. They may have some left if you call."

Carly thought about it for a moment. With an excuse already forming, she found herself nodding. "Maybe I will."

What else did she have to do? And she had always wanted to go. It could be an adventure.

"Excuse me," a male voice said from behind Carly.

She turned to see the man who had been staring at her from the bar. Seeing him up close and hearing his voice, her jaw dropped open when she realized who he was.

"Eddie?" she exclaimed. Eddie was Emily's ex-husband, the alcoholic she had left two years ago, returning to Bon Chance.

"Yes. Carly, right? Emily's friend? Do you mind if I speak to you for a moment?" He hesitated a moment. "Alone?"

Carly looked to the rest of the group, who had obviously figured out who he was by the looks on their faces. "Yeah, I guess."

Carly followed him out the side doors to the patio area where a few customers sat around wrought iron tables.

She watched as Eddie fidgeted, his feet shuffling.

"So, um, how is Emily?"

"She's good."

He smiled. "Good. Good for her."

He took a deep breath, exhaled, and looked up at the night sky. "I'm sober now. Have been since I made an ass out of myself when I went down there for that cook-off. I could kick Justice and Jeremy for bringing me down there, but ultimately it was me who is responsible."

Carly chewed her bottom lip, unsure of what to say. This was the last thing she expected him to say when they came outside.

"I've wanted to call Emily," he continued. "Make amends, as they say. My sponsor says I should, but I just can't bring myself to do it. Maybe one of these days..."

"Maybe you should. I think she would understand," Carly said. She would probably be as stunned as Carly was at the moment, but Emily had never been one to hold grudges and at one time had loved Eddie. It would probably give her some peace. "I'll tell her I ran into you. Do you want to give me your number?"

He smiled. He was really attractive with his eyes clear, and his speech not all slurred. "Yes."

Carly punched the numbers into her phone and saved them. "I guess I should get back in."

"Yeah, I think the music is about to start. Enjoy. Ron, the guy who does karaoke, is really good. I come most weekends"

"My friends were telling me how good he is. I'm looking forward to it."

The music came on as they walked back into the bar. The karaoke guy played a couple of songs while he got set up, and Carly and the group made small talk.

Gemma reached for Carly's hand. "He's about to sing."

Carly turned to watch the slender man grab the microphone, and she was transfixed as he sang a song about being fired away.

"I don't like country music, but I like this song," Carly said. "He sings it better than that other guy." His singing was smooth and silky and as good as any singer she'd heard on the radio.

"He sings with a band called Broken Meauxjo. It's more rock. That might be more your speed. We can go listen to them one night if you'd like," Gemma said.

Carly thought of all the bands she'd had play at Snapper's. It was one of the favorite parts of her job, booking the bands, then enjoying watching them perform. She loved live music. And she was actually supposed to be looking for bands for the café.

"Sure."

"This music makes me want to dance. Care to take a turn on the dance floor with me?" Lucky asked.

"Lucky, I told you, I can't dance."

"Oh, come on, *cher*. It's a slow one. The worst you can do is step on my toes, and I wore my boots tonight, so I think I'm safe."

He smiled at her, and she found herself standing. The man really was too much.

The dance floor was in an area that was sunken in. A couple of steps down, and they were standing in front of the small raised area used as a stage. Jasper and Gemma followed them.

"Now, those two?" Lucky said as he pulled Carly close and started to move, "they are great dancers together. They put Ryder and his partners to shame."

He was a smooth dancer himself, and Carly found it very easy to relax and follow his lead. He tugged her a little closer, but not so close as to be too intimate. The embrace and the feel of his arms around her comforted her, and she rested her head on his shoulder.

For tonight, she would forget about leaving her world behind.

Chapter Twenty-One

CARLY SLID THE ROUND white sunglasses down over her eyes as she stepped out of her car. She could already hear the accordion music even though she had parked about two blocks away. Gibson had given her some parking area guidance, and she had been able to find a spot that wasn't too far from the park.

The sun was warm on her face as she walked the short distance to the festival. Canopies in various shades dotted the hilly landscape, ready to provide shelter as the day progressed. Some even had thrift store couches that would be good for a little cat-nap when the sun got too hot or the drinks were too many.

It was early Sunday afternoon and the crowd, though light, was steady. She stopped at one of the signs located at a crossing area to locate the main stage and began making her way along, taking in all the sights. People of all ages were gathering for the day's festivities, from babies still in strollers, to the older generation with gentlemen in "gimmie" hats and ladies in faux pearls.

There were only four stages, so the main stage was easy to find, as was the huge white canopied beer tent. She smiled at the sign encouraging patrons to tip and donate to the local writing project for students. She smiled when she recognized Dawn as she walked up.

"Hey!" Dawn said, "you made it."

"I did. It's a gorgeous day today."

"You are going to love it."

"I already do. This is amazing. And it happens every year?"

"Yep. You have to be sure to check it all out." Dawn started pointing in different directions. "If you head over that way, you'll find the food vendors. That's a good way to sample local restaurants all in one place. Keep walking that way, and you'll find the local artists. I always manage to pick up a piece or two. Are you staying here, by the way? Or just helping your friend out?"

Carly chewed her bottom lip a moment before responding with a shrug and a shake of her head. "I'm going to be staying for a bit."

"We're glad to have you." Dawn's attention was nabbed by Dylan, who had just arrived. He greeted Dawn with a hug and a smile for Carly. "It's great to see you. Are you here to help?"

Dawn nudged him with her elbow. "This is her first festival. Let her go enjoy it. We'll twist her arm next year."

"You got it."

"Oh, I never asked you if you wanted something to drink." Dawn laughed. "I'm a terrible bartender. I don't know why Dylan keeps me here."

"Free labor," he muttered, to which he received another poke.

"A Bud Light, please."

"You got it." She turned and fished a blue can out of the huge tubs of ice and handed it to Carly.

"Oh, I forgot to get tickets. Hang on."

"Girl, I'll get this one. You can buy me one tomorrow when we meet to go over your work."

"Sounds like a plan to me."

More patrons began lining up, so Carly said her goodbyes to them both and turned in the direction of the food tents, which, honestly, she didn't need to follow any map to, only her nose.

After walking up one side and down the other, reading all the menus that listed items like crawfish and spinach boats, jambalaya, and etouffee, she finally decided on alligator on a stick, bits of battered and fried gator on a shish kebab style stick.

She found the stage where Geno Delafosse was scheduled to play and settled down on the edge of a pavilion. The concrete set up a few inches to provide a bit of a seat. She looked at the crowd, envying those who had brought comfortable chairs with cup holders. *Next year*. And she would be back next year. Maybe she could get Gabe and Grace to come in as well. Even if she wasn't living here, she could always make plans for travel. *Travel*. Other than coming here, she hadn't been out of Bon Chance since she left A.J. in Biloxi. Well, there were the occasional trips to New Orleans, but that was hardly considered "traveling."

Finished with her food and drink, she stood and threw the trash away. She took some red tickets she had purchased after her visit to Dawn out of her back pocket and headed for the beer tent.

"Hey, *cher*," she heard as she started to step in line. Recognizing the voice, she smiled.

"Hey, Lucky. You didn't say anything about coming when I saw you last night."

"Ah, it was a last-minute decision. My brother Julien wanted to come. You should come meet him."

"I'd like that. Just gimme a sec."

"I'll stay right here."

When she returned, Lucky threw an arm around her shoulder.

"This is one of my favorite festivals around. I love the music. And it's not all crowded like some of the other ones."

"I'm enjoying it so far. Of course, I've only been here about an hour."

He maneuvered her to the edge of the crowd, and she spotted Julien immediately. "Oh, my God! There *are* two of you."

Lucky flashed her a dimpled grin and nodded. "Oh, yeah. But, like I said, I'm the better looking one."

From where Carly was standing, she couldn't tell. They were mirror images of each other. Even had some of the same mannerisms.

Double Trouble for sure.

"Julien," Lucky said, "this is Carly. Ryder's friend."

"Oh, awesome! It's great to meet you. I've heard Ryder talk about you a time or two. We really need to get down to that town he was telling us about. And that bar, what was it? Snapper's?"

Carly winced.

Lucky, noticing, was quick to respond. "I don't know about all that. But we could drive down there one weekend to see him in Biloxi. Do a little gambling. Check out the scene."

"That, my brother, sounds like a plan. Let's make it happen."

"How about you? You up for a trip? We can take the bike," he said to Carly.

"Uh, I don't know. Biloxi..."

"Oh, don't tell me. You broke a man's heart and can't go back now?"

"I wouldn't say that." Carly laughed, thinking of throwing her fiancé's mistress's expensive shoes from the Biloxi bridge when she left Biloxi the last time.

"I'm sure whatever it was, it's all water under the bridge now."

"I'm quite sure it is." *Well, something was in the water under the bridge now.*

The band playing on the stage took a bow and began to disassemble their instruments. While they worked, a man came out to make the introductions for the next band, Geno Delafosse and the French Rockin' Boogie.

"Oh, I love this band!" Carly exclaimed. "Especially the chicken song."

"They're some of my favorites too. I try to catch them whenever they play locally. You going to dance?"

"No, you know, I think I'll leave that up to you this time. I think I might find a little spot and jot some of this down. It's too perfect not to use it as some inspiration."

"You do that."

Carly gave him a quick hug. "I'll come back around and see if I can find you."

"I will look forward to that, *cher*."

Carly walked around the dancing area back to where she had been sitting before. She plopped down Indian style with her beer tucked beside her. She fished a marker out of her purse and grabbed the only thing she had to write on, the festival brochure.

Enjoying the feel of the sun on her face and the sound of the band who had just began to play, Carly began writing.

Sunshine

Joy
Charming men
Ladies dancing
People with dogs
Young girls who smell like pot
Smiles—the band, the people
Cold beer
Hot day
Sunshine
Joy

Chapter Twenty-Two

CARLY WALKED NERVOUSLY into the fenced area of the Beer Garden off Jefferson Street. It was a gorgeous day to be outside and surrounded by the pots of hanging red, yellow, and pink flowers.

Dawn had sent her a text earlier, asking to meet her here. She had finished *All I Want for Christmas* and was ready to return it, with her remarks.

Carly felt the nerves all the way to the pit of her stomach. She had no idea what Dawn would say. Would she like it? Love it? She didn't know what she would do if Dawn hated it. What would she do then? She had worked on this story so long it seemed to have become a part of her. Maybe too much.

She ordered a beer and resisted the urge to get a shot, if only to tame the fear that gnawed at her. It was one thing to have Daniel read and critique her work. It was an entirely different thing to have another author look at her stuff. A bestselling author, at that.

This was her moment of truth.

Dawn was seated at one of the picnic tables, her dog Chance, a.k.a. the Devil Dog, seated beside her on the ground. His little black and white head rested on his paws. She wished she would have brought Sammy, but she'd been so distracted, she hadn't really thought about it.

Dawn smiled when she saw Carly. "Hi, Carly!"

"Hey!"

Carly slid onto the wooden bench across from Dawn, who asked, "Do you want to exchange pleasantries? Or do you want to talk about the book?"

"The book, please," Carly said.

Dawn laughed. "I thought as much. Do you want the good news first or the bad?"

Bad news? There was bad? How bad?

Dawn must have read the panic on her face because she was quick to respond. "Calm down. It's not that bad. Have you ever had your work critiqued before?"

"By a friend."

"Ah...Sometimes it's best to get a fresh eye from someone else. It helps me. Speaking of which, we do have that group that gets together a couple of times a month, and we drink a few drinks and talk about writing. Dylan is a member. You should come."

Great, bad news and a critique suggestion. My writing does suck.

Dawn took the manuscript out of her backpack and handed it to Carly. "I've made some comments here and there that you can look at when you want to. Overall, you've got some writing chops. You have a funny voice, and a natural way of writing that drew me in."

Carly relaxed; it couldn't be that bad.

"But there's not a lot going on in this story. She's looking for a man and going on dates. Funny stuff. That's pretty common in romance, but there's not a lot of 'meat' to the story. There's very limited conflict, that thing that makes people want to keep reading. Why does she keep choosing the wrong man?

What makes your character tick? Make me care about what happens to her. Give me some tension. Give me some *why*."

"Why?"

"Yeah, why do I care about this character? Why do I want to keep reading? My honest opinion?"

"Please."

"You're too close to this story. Give yourself a break from it. Doodle something else. Talk to people. Listen to conversations. Listen to great music. I'm challenging you today to bring something new to our next writers group meeting. It will get you used to sharing your work in front of other people."

She knew Dawn was right. It hurt to hear, but deep-down, Carly knew her biggest obstacle was fear. She was afraid of exposing herself to others through her writing.

"How do you do it?" Carly asked. "How do you put your work out there for others to read?"

"It scared me senseless the first time." Dawn grinned. "Especially the sexy scenes. But you get used to it. And you realize your readers know that just because you write something, it doesn't mean it's about *you*. It's not all about *you*, Carly. It's about your characters. What they want. Bottom line? It's not bad. But it's not great either."

"Ouch." Carly flinched.

Dawn tapped the manuscript. "I would be doing you an injustice if I told you what you wanted to hear. Come to our group next time. I promise you'll get a lot out of it. Bring something new if you want."

Carly nodded. It had been awhile since she had written anything new. She'd been so engrossed in this story, so determined to make it work, she'd shoved all other ideas aside. It was time to try something else. To throw herself into another project. Which seemed to be the story of her life these days.

Personal growth really sucked sometimes.

Chapter Twenty-Three

CARLY PRIED ONE EYE open as the alarm on her phone started to ring.

5:00 a.m.

What in the world had possessed her to volunteer to help Lucky cook today? As she started to shift around in bed to get up, a steady thumping reminded her.

The dogs.

Proceeds from the cook-off would go to help the veterinary clinic raise money for rescue animals. Lucky had told her they would have some adoptable pets there for people to see and hopefully take to their forever homes.

She gave Sammy a pat on the head. "Come on, girl, get up. It's for a good cause."

Half an hour later, she was showered and sitting at the small bistro table with a cup of coffee and a sausage biscuit she had heated in the microwave. She scrolled through social media while she munched and waited for Lucky to come pick her up.

Abbeville, he'd said this town was. She'd looked it up on the map, and it wasn't too far. Looked like a little town in the country.

When they arrived about an hour later, she was not wrong. It was a small town with only one main highway running through it. The sun had just risen when they pulled into a parking space and began to unload the pots, pans, burners, and tents he would need to cook that day. His brother Julien had come along too, and the two of them were hauling the heavy stuff.

Carly helped with the various tablecloths, big plastic storage containers, and coolers.

She was impressed to see an entire block had been set aside just for cooks. Setting up on the outer edges would be local artists and vendors. It looked like this event would be very successful in raising funds and awareness for rescued animals.

A volunteer with a Whittington Veterinary Clinic tag welcomed them as they began to set up and gave them important information about restroom locations, where the beer tent would be, and what time the food would need to be ready for taste testing.

People attending could buy an armband and taste all the food and vote for their favorite as well, so there would be multiple awards given out.

Lucky set up the burner and put on a big silver pot. "Let's get this done. Carly, you're on roux duty, just like we practiced. Julien and I will chop and season the meats."

Julien grabbed a few bottles of water out of the cooler and tossed one to each of them. "For now, we hydrate."

The morning zoomed by as the three worked to prepare the gumbo. And despite the sausage biscuit Carly had had earlier, her stomach growled as all the different smells began to mingle in the air.

Lucky lifted his ball cap and wiped his brow. "All done. Now we just gotta let it cook and do its thing. Hand me a beer, my brother. I've worked up quite a thirst."

Julien pulled three ice cold bottles out of the cooler he was using as a seat.

"That gumbo smells incredible," Carly said. "I think we have a winner on our hands."

"Oh, you think so?"

"I definitely do."

Lucky grinned. "We'll just have to see."

"So, this is the 'Anything Over Rice Cook-Off'? What are some things you think they are cooking?" Carly gestured around the cooking area.

"Who knows? Fish, shrimp, rabbit, maybe some turtle."

"I have to check this out. I want to try everything!"

"Get you a wristband. We got things covered here. Walk around. They'll start bringing the dogs out on stage later." He nodded over to the stage area where a musician was playing some old southern rock.

Carly grabbed her backpack and set off to see the sights, a smile on her face.

• • • •

JOEY WALKED THROUGH the crowded streets of the French Quarter with Noah. The two had driven up that morning to look at some apartments. They had been through several buildings and rental houses.

"Man, rent here is high, and the places are small and old. That last one had only enough room for a mini fridge. Can you imagine? How would I keep stuff to cook in that?" Joey said.

"It's no Bon Chance, I'll tell you that," Noah said. "Too many buildings and people for me. Then the heat in the summer. Not only do you suffocate, it stinks. Literally."

"It's not permanent. School only lasts a year. But who knows? I may get a job here. I'd really prefer something coastal."

"Why don't you look for something near the beach?"

"I'd have to move."

"And?"

"That would be weird."

"Now you sound like Carly. Have you talked to my sister, by the way?"

Joey's heart constricted. "I have. She's not coming back any time soon."

Noah nodded. "Good for her. It's time. She's been dependent on us way too long. We were all just too comfortable, I guess."

"Yeah. Funny how life makes you uncomfortable sometimes. She did send me some pics from a festival she went to. She had some gator on a stick. And a few band pics. It looked like a lot fun. Nothing you would see around Bon Chance. Just fishing and stuff there. And she's doing some cook-off today. With that guy."

"Carly's cooking? I'm impressed. It may be good for her, though."

"I know," Joey said, stopping to look through the window of a tourist trap souvenir shop. Mardi Gras music blared from the open door. "It just sucks."

"Carly gone or this music?" Noah grabbed his arm. "Come on, let's go in. We'll buy her a stupid t-shirt and a shot glass and send her a NOLA care package. We'll make her laugh. She'll love it."

Joey looked up at a pink shirt that had the image of oysters with the words "Shuck Me" on it. "Oh, yeah. That sounds like a plan. The goofier the better." His spirits lifted, and he followed his friend into the store.

• • • •

CARLY SAT CROSS-LEGGED on a hay bale off to the right of the stage. The band had switched to a local swamp pop group, and she was sitting in the sun enjoying the music. She could get used to living in Lafayette if there was something like this going on every weekend. Always somewhere to go, something new to see. It was a brand-new adventure, and she wanted to take full advantage of it.

She watched as a twenty-something guy asked a woman to dance. The woman smiled and accepted his hand. Feeling inspired, Carly reached into her backpack for her pen and paper.

She sketched out a few lines.

The October sun was warm against my face.
I looked across the dance area.
It was him.
Would he ask me to dance?
How I wanted him to.
He's heading this way!
The answer, of course, was yes.

Carly smiled and tucked the notebook back into her bag. She needed to head back to the tent. It was almost time to judge, but in Carly's opinion, today was already a win.

Chapter Twenty-Four

DECEMBER 20TH

"Bells will be ringing." I sing along with Wayne Toups as I put another gold fleur de lis ornament on Glinda's enormous Christmas tree.

Glinda is across the room decorating the buffet with a smaller tree and pine garland. She is singing along as well. With my parents living in Florida now, I had started helping Glinda with her decorations a few seasons ago. As much as I love Christmas, I don't put up a tree in my small cabin. Apartments in Bon Chance are scarce, it being mostly fishing camps and small family homes, so I had taken up residence in one of Glinda's cabins. I pay a small monthly rent and get free meals. It's perfect for me.

"Heard from your parents?" Glinda asks.

"I talked to Mom yesterday. Noah is scheduled to be in, and Ben will be in from his twenty-eight- day stint. I'm so excited! We'll all be together this year."

"I bet you are. When are you leaving?"

"A couple of days before Christmas."

"That's good. Gabriel called me as well. He's coming in for a couple of days. He can't stay long. He's still trying to work and play in the band. They're not getting enough gigs to completely pay the bills yet, so he's doing both. Poor thing, I think he's worn out."

"I bet," I say. Gabriel had moved to Austin with his friends, Bennett and Nate. The music scene was hopping there, they said, and they wanted to take advantage of it. I kept in touch with him on Facebook and enjoyed seeing the pics he posted of the three of them playing music together.

I put the last of the ornaments on the tree and dust my hands off on my jeans.

"You ready for some hot chocolate and porch sitting?" Glinda asks. "I'm about ready for a break myself."

"Sure." I call for Sammy, who is dozing by the unlit fireplace. It wouldn't be cool enough for a fire until the sun went down, if then. But a dog could dream, I guess.

Sammy and I go outside, and I take a seat in one of the huge white rocking chairs that adorn the wide porch. I had given up asking Glinda if she needed help in the kitchen a long time ago. Not that she wanted my help, anyway, considering my kitchen skills. I've been known to mess up hot chocolate. I am looking out at the calm water of the gulf when Glinda comes outside to join me.

"Here you go, dear," Glinda says, laying the tray on the table between the two rocking chairs. The two mugs on the tray read "Peace, Love, Joy, and Gumbo" and they're decorated with dancing crawfish.

I take one of the steaming mugs filled with Glinda's own mix of hot chocolate and covered with whipped cream. I take a slow sip, closing my eyes as the warm goodness hits my tongue.

"Wonderful as always, Aunt Glinda."

"I got some mix ready for you to take home. Don't be tryin' to make it with milk like you did the last time."

I grimace. Feeling adventurous last year, I had decided to make hot chocolate with milk like Glinda did and ended up scorching and ruining my pan. The cabin smelled awful too.

"I'll leave that up to you."

"Good deal," she says, sipping from her own mug. *"Now, tell me all about your book and how the dating is going. Any prospects?"*

"I don't know, Glinda," I say, exhaling a deep breath.

"That doesn't sound good."

"I heard that," I say, and she laughs. *"What do you think about butterflies?"* I ask. Butterflies have been on my mind a lot lately.

"Well, I think they're pretty. Don't see them too much this time of year."

"That's not what I mean. I mean the kind you feel when you meet someone. That little feeling you get in your stomach."

Glinda smiles. *"Of course, dear. I know. Just playin' with you. What do* you *think about butterflies?"*

"I don't know, Glinda. I'm beginning to think that fluttering might be a sign that I need to run."

"Could be gas," Glinda says under her breath.

"This isn't funny."

"I know, dear." She pats my hand. *"Keep going."*

"Which do you think is better? A relationship that starts with butterflies or one that starts with stability and trust?"

"Carly, I'm way too old to be playing around in the yard with butterflies. I think stability and trust, but that's me. You need to find the answer for yourself."

"Joey doesn't give me butterflies. He makes me smile. And we're always honest with each other. Is that like stability and trust?"

"What do you think?"

"I don't really know. Ryder gave me butterflies."

"Is that right?"

"Yeah, but I haven't seen him in a few days. His being gone hasn't made my heart grow fonder, though. I just miss him. His presence, his smile, and that goofy growl sound he makes in my ear."

Jack still gives me butterflies. His voice on his voicemail does it. When I picture his smile or his blue eyes, I get the chills.

"You want to know what I really think, Carly?"

"Yes, what do you really think?"

"I think you're young, and beautiful, and vivacious. And I think you're spending way too much time worrying about this. When it's time, it will happen, and you will know."

I frown because that really isn't the answer I wanted.

But it was the answer I got.

• • • •

CARLY AND LUCKY WALKED into the bar, where eighties music was pounding from the speakers.

"This is my kind of place already," Carly said.

They took seats at the long bar. There were several spots open, as it was still early. They ordered drinks, and Carly sat back to take in the surroundings.

"I can't believe this place is here." They had decided to celebrate their cook-off win with some live music. They were at some place almost in the middle of nowhere, although Carly could see the lights of more establishments as they had turned into the parking lot.

"They have oysters on Wednesdays," Lucky said.

"I love oysters," Carly replied.

"Maybe I'll just have to bring you around sometime. But I won't be held responsible if they get you all frisky."

"Oh, that's an old wives' tale."

His eyes sparkled. Carly once again felt that little stirring in her stomach. He took a step closer, his body touching hers. He reached around her to grab his beer. After taking a long drink, he winked. "Is it?"

Gemma and Jasper would be meeting them later. They had stopped for dinner. "Date night," Lucky had said.

The same guy Carly had loved for his karaoke singing came in. He shook hands with Lucky, who introduced her to him. "This is Ron. Ron, Carly."

"Nice to meet you. You did a wonderful job at karaoke."

He smiled. "Thank you."

Talked to turned to fishing, and they began comparing notes on the latest tournaments, what was biting where, and at that point, Carly's attention returned to the bar. It was a huge building. The bar was in the front, the stage and dance floor in the back. It had an assortment of high top and picnic tables. Pictures of musicians lined the walls. The band had already set up, the drum set proudly displaying the name "Broken Mojeaux."

If that wasn't a metaphor for her life, Carly didn't know what was. If anyone's mojeaux was broken, it was hers.

She thought of the manuscript Dawn had returned to her, still laying on her kitchen table unopened. She was too afraid to open it now. Afraid of the comments and more afraid because she knew Dawn was right.

Carly exhaled a deep breath. She'd get back to her writing. Her mojo would come back, and things would return to normal. Well, she smiled to herself, as normal as life was for her.

"Whatcha smilin' about, *cher*?" Lucky chucked her on the chin.

"Life."

"Oh? Why don't we celebrate with a little dance?"

He held out his hand, and Carly gladly took it.

When the music turned from eighties pop to a slow country song about being freedom and traveling the country in an old van, Carly grinned and stepped into Lucky's embrace. After being tied down with the business, freedom and traveling in an old van or on a motorcycle sounded like a damn good idea.

"Lucky?" She leaned back a bit to see his face.

"Yes?" His smile made the butterflies in her stomach flutter.

"Let's take that trip to Biloxi. You said we could take the bike, right?"

"You betcha."

Carly thought of traveling down the coast with the wind in her hair and the sun on her face. "Count me in."

"I'll get with Julien, and we'll make a plan. Next weekend is Halloween. How about the weekend after?"

"That sounds perfect."

He hugged her tightly for a moment. "We're going to have a good time, *cher*. Just you, me, the bike, and the ocean."

She closed her eyes and pictured it. "I can only imagine."

She rested her head on his shoulder, and they finished the dance.

Chapter Twenty-Five

CARLY CHECKED THE HEAT of the charcoal just as Lucky had shown her at Turtles. It felt pretty close to what it should, so she slid the burgers onto the grill. She had put too many on there for just her, but that was how they came. Apparently, no one just cooked for themselves. She had too many patties and too many buns. But she was doing a happy dance anyway. She was cooking.

She would have leftovers for tomorrow, and she was sure Sammy would love a burger instead of dry dog food.

She resumed her seat on the bottom step of the apartments with her notebook in her lap. Sammy walked around the small yard, nose to the ground, tracking all the animals that had dared traipse through her space that day.

She tucked earbuds in and keyed on the song that had played while she and Lucky had danced the night before. It had been stuck in her head all day long, so she figured she'd see if she could use it for inspiration.

Her head bobbed softly to the rhythm, and images and a story slowly began to take shape.

She grabbed the keys to her ancient VW Bug convertible. She tossed a worn-out suitcase onto the back seat and hopped in. She started the car and backed out of the driveway. Destination? Unknown.

She was free.

She longed to see the stars on the ocean while she sat beside a warm fire. Just her and her guitar.

A gypsy soul, her grandmother had said. But Grannie was gone now, her body free from the disease that had taken her life. Grannie's last words to her had been, "Be free, Gypsy. Go see everything I wanted to see. Write your songs. I don't have a lot of money, but what I have is yours."

The wind from the highway dried the tears as they fell.

"We're free, Grannie. We're finally free."

The song ended, and Carly pulled the earbuds out and read what she had just sketched out.

"Damn," she said aloud. "That's definitely not *How to find a Boyfriend*."

She chewed on the end of the pen. Now, who was Gypsy and what did she want? And what was she finally free from?

. . . .

A FEW NIGHTS LATER, Gibson opened Dawn's door after Carly knocked. "Come on in," he said.

Carly followed him through the house, a cute little Craftsman style. It was older but had been completely and recently redone.

Dawn was putting the finishing touches on an elaborate charcuterie board she placed in the middle of the raised bar. She took an extra slice of cheese and handed it down to Chance, who was standing at attention, waiting on the treat.

"Carly! It's so nice that you could come. Have a glass of wine." She gestured to the collection of bottles of white and red. Carly grabbed one of the glasses and poured herself some white.

"Are there a lot of people coming?" Carly asked, hoping the answer was no.

"No, not really. We like to keep our group small and intimate. It allows for more time to share."

Carly breathed a sigh of relief. The thought of a whole room full of people reading what she wrote made her stomach flutter. And not in a good way.

"Oh, good. I did bring a little piece I'm working on."

"Great. Grab a little snack. We're waiting on Dylan."

"We're always waiting on Dylan," Gibson chimed in, laughing.

"I swear, one of these days I'm going to write a book titled *Waiting on Dylan*."

Carly took her wineglass and sat at the bar. She nibbled on the various appetizers Dawn had out.

"This is your first time here. Would you like me to show you around?" Dawn asked.

"That would be great."

Dawn took her on a tour through her house, which looked surprisingly normal for someone who wrote about vampires and haunted hotels in New Orleans. There was a fair amount of artwork and photographs depicting scenes from the French Quarter.

When Dawn opened the door to her office, Carly resisted the urge to gasp.

"Excuse the mess. I have a work in progress."

Mess? Carly thought. This was beautiful chaos. There was a storyboard on the wall, with different colored Post-it notes. More notes littered the desk, separated into what looked like groups. What amazed Carly the most was the cover posters that competed for wall space.

She walked over to the set of three frames and reached out to touch them.

"Gorgeous, huh? My cover designer is amazing."

"They're incredible." Carly turned. "This right here is what I want. I want to write. I want to be published, and I want my own cover poster."

"Then do it. Dawn shrugged. "You have the talent. Stop playing around and write words that mean something."

Carly felt tears prick the back of her eyelids. Here she was, standing in the office of a bestselling novelist. A writer who believed she could do it.

Dawn smiled and put a hand on her shoulder. "Now, come on. Let's have some wine and talk writing."

"Let's do it. I think it's time."

As Dawn closed the door behind them, Carly knew another door had just opened.

Chapter Twenty-Six

CARLY GRABBED THE SILVER pan of the small cheese-cakes she had made for Dawn's Halloween party from the fridge. She couldn't wait to show off the creations she had found on Pinterest, mini cherry cheesecakes with an eyeball gumball in the center. "Bloody Eyeball Cheesecakes," they were called. They were gross and cute at the same time.

It was the first time she had ever brought food to a party. Usually, she brought drinks and ice. She had taken a picture and sent to Emily earlier. Emily had told her she needed to make some for the café. Carly didn't know if she was ready for all that, but if they went over well at the party, maybe she'd give it a try.

She took a moment to check out her make-up in the re-flection from the glass fronted cabinets. Normally, she went as some kind of zombie for Halloween. This year, she had cho-sen an eighties theme. She had teased her blonde hair, sprayed some hot pink hair spray in it, and used her neon colored eye-shadows.

Lucky would be there soon to pick her up. She couldn't be-lieve he had agreed to go with her. It didn't seem to be his kind of thing, but she was glad he was coming. Gibson would be there as well, so there would be another familiar face.

She knew Dawn, but she had no idea who else would be there. Dylan, of course. Carly couldn't wait to see what the two of them would wear. Would Dawn dress as one of her vam-pire characters? The possibility was the reason Carly herself had chosen something else.

Her cell phone dinged. It was Lucky; he was five minutes away. She wondered if he was dressing up. He hadn't said when Dawn had invited them both at Legends during happy hour a week ago.

She put the top back on the silver pan, adjusted her costume, and after a pat to Sammy's head, went to wait on the porch.

• • • •

LUCKY ADJUSTED THE cheap black wig he had bought at Wal-Mart earlier. He had waited too long for a costume and had to get creative. He felt like a fool. He hadn't dressed up for Halloween since his college days, and then it had always been something cheesy, like a toga, or doctor.

There was something about Carly, though, that made him want to see her smile. If this costume didn't make her laugh, he had definitely lost his touch.

He checked his reflection in the mirror, making sure the wig was on just right, and straightened the collar on his purple shirt, and grabbed the gaming headset he had borrowed from Julien earlier, and headed out to pick up Carly.

• • • •

CARLY SLID INTO LUCKY'S truck, and after adjusting the tray of cheesecakes on the seat between them, she finally looked at him. In the dim light of the truck, she could see his black wig and purple shirt.

"I don't get it," she said, cocking her head to one side.

"Blauahamdhaibm, Geaux Tigahs!" he said, donning the headset.

The realization hit, and she started laughing. "No," she finally said, gasping. "You didn't dress up as Coach Orgeron."

"Yes, ma'am. Tiger football, baby! And you? Olivia Newton John? No black leather pantsuit?"

"Yeah, like I have one of those just hanging in the closet. I'm just your average eighties teen."

"That's where you're wrong."

"Oh, why?"

He reached out and ran a finger along her jawbone, causing her to shiver, those butterflies fluttering around again. She cleared her throat and looked away from those bright blue eyes of his.

His voice slightly lower, he said, "There's nothing average about you."

Carly swallowed hard, hoping to drown those damn butterflies. That was the last thing she needed.

"So, you should see the cheesecakes I made." The nervous babbling began. "They are so cute. Well, not really cute, like cute. More like scary cute." *Oh, my God.* "Please just turn the music up."

He chuckled low. "You got it."

He turned up the radio he had streaming from his phone, and together they sang the song *Monster Mash* as they drove to Dawn's house.

• • • •

"SO, YOU AND LUCKY ARE going to Biloxi next weekend?" Dawn asked. Dawn had dressed up like a vampire, and Carly was not disappointed. Not only was she a vamp, she was dressed as a flapper in a little black dress, headdress, pearls, and a long white cigarette holder.

"Yes. He talked me into it."

"That man is fine. It wouldn't take much convincing for me," Dawn teased.

"It's not like that. We're just friends."

"Oh, right."

"Girl, I don't need that. I'm in Lafayette to be single and independent. To do things on my own for a change."

"I didn't say marry the man. But if I was in your shoes, I'd definitely not waste an opportunity." She winked.

At the mention of shoes, Carly's mind flashed back to the red shoes she'd found on the floor of her fiancé's apartment. Why, she had no idea. Maybe it was the idea of returning to Biloxi after all this time. Would she run into A.J.? If so, what would she do?

"Uh-oh. I don't like that look. This is a party." Dawn smiled and slung her pearls around in a circle. "Let me get us another drink. Maybe I'll get you to dance the Thriller dance with me later."

"Really?"

"It's that or the Time Warp."

Carly shook her head. "It's going to take more than one drink to get me to do either one."

"Then, let's get started." Dawn hooked her arm around Carly's, and they headed off to the kitchen for more Witches' Brew.

Chapter Twenty-Seven

CARLY WAITED NERVOUSLY on the porch, rocking back and forth in the chair to try to quiet her nerves. She would chat with Sammy, but the dog was staying with Gemma, Jasper, Duke, and their two dogs, Annie and Cheauxnuff. She wondered how Sammy would take to the temporary surroundings, but Gemma had assured her Sammy was doing fine.

"Ruling the roost," Gemma had said. Carly had not been surprised.

Lucky would be pulling up soon, and while she was excited to take the trip, she was worried about being in such close quarters with a man she was so attracted to.

Joey had been quiet since she'd told him she was going with Lucky. That only added to her trepidation. But Joey was in Bon Chance, and Carly wasn't ready to go back yet. The wound of losing the bar was still too fresh. How could she go back and pretend everything was normal when it wasn't?

That was why this trip was such a great idea. It had been years since she'd been, not since she'd lived in Biloxi with A.J. She'd worked so much at the hotel back then that she hadn't gone as often as she would have liked.

She was looking forward to watching the sunrise on the beach. She'd lived in Bon Chance for years and had taken the sunrise for granted. She'd usually been crawling into bed a little before the sun rose after closing the bar. She'd become more of a night owl than an early bird.

She heard a motorcycle round the corner off Congress and checked the time. That had to be Lucky. Grabbing one last sip of coffee, she went into the apartment to gather her things.

She was still eyeing the small bag she'd packed when Lucky's loud footsteps sounded on the porch. She'd left the screen door open, and seeing her in the living room, he came inside.

"What's wrong?" he asked.

"I don't know if I brought enough stuff."

"You do realize we're traveling on a Harley, right? And we're only staying two days?

She nodded. "But..."

"Just bring what you've got. If you need anything else, we'll buy it."

He reached out and tugged her ponytail. "Stop worrying and come on. We have some riding to do, and this weather is perfect. If we hit the road now, we can stop by one of my favorite places to eat before they get too packed. You're going to love their margaritas. And the oysters are great too."

Carly grinned. "Now, you're speaking my language. Let's hit the road."

He grabbed her traveling bag, and after locking up, Carly joined him in the driveway. He secured her bag in the storage area and handed her a helmet. "Safety first."

He helped her with the chin straps then swung his leg over the bike.

"Hop on, my lady. Then just enjoy the ride."

She climbed on behind him as he put his own helmet on. He switched the radio on, and Kenny Chesney's *No Shirt, No Shoes, No Problems* started playing.

Thoughts of Lucky with no shirt on danced around in her head as she reached out and put her hands on his sides to steady herself as they took off.

She felt the muscles of his waist tighten as she touched him, and her brain went haywire.

This may be a long trip.

• • • •

THEY PULLED OFF THE interstate in Gulfport and into the parking lot of a seafood restaurant. Before going in, Carly stopped to take a few touristy pictures of the huge pink chair and the shack-style décor.

It was just after eleven, and already the parking lot was starting to fill. Carly relished every moment, from the feel of the salty coast air on her face, to the sun that beat down on her head and warmed her cheeks.

The hostess was quick to seat them out on the back deck where they had a view of the sandy beach and the boats that traveled on the calm water.

"You have to have the oysters. They just taste better here by the water."

"That sounds good."

Soon, the beverages were delivered, and Carly leaned back against her chair

"So, Miss Carly, what else would you like to do on your little getaway?'

"I want to walk on the beach and watch the sunrise."

"There's only one time I like to see the sun rise, and that's after I spend a satisfying evening."

Carly swiped her napkin at him. "There will be none of that." She batted her eyelashes at him. "I have a reputation to protect."

"I've heard all about your reputation."

Carly shook her head. "You've heard no such thing." She took another sip of her drink. "Seriously, though, I'm trying to decide if I want to go to the Sea Treasure Casino or not."

"Why wouldn't you?"

"My ex-fiancé's family owns it, and he's usually there on the weekends."

"Ex-fiancé?" He raised an eyebrow. "How long has that been?"

"Three years."

"*Cher*, you gotta let that go. I don't know what he did, but looks to me like you're better off without him."

The red shoes flashed in her mind again, and the vision of A.J. and his mistress in their bed. "I caught him cheating. Red-handed."

"So, he's an asshole. Let's get all dressed up, go to the casino, and have ourselves a good time. The way I see it, we're here to pass a good time, and that's exactly what we're going to do." He gave her a wicked grin. "Besides, if we run into him, I'll just pretend you're my fiancée and we're so in love."

"Let's just not think of him. We're here, the weather is beautiful, and we have oysters on the way."

He nodded. "That's my girl."

• • • •

"CALM DOWN, CARLY," Lucky said. "You may not even see him, anyway. This is a big casino." He leaned against the bar, facing toward the buzzing and cacophony of the slot machines.

"Oh, he'll be out and about. It's Saturday night. He'll be looking for his next ruby-slippered harlot."

"Come on, now. Leave Dorothy out of this."

"You're right. More like the witch the house fell on."

He laughed. "Now you're talking."

She took a deep breath and pulled on the skirt that felt just a bit too short. "Are you sure I look okay?"

His eyes clouded, and he looked away.

"I don't. Oh, my God! Let's go back so I can change."

"Carly, you are gorgeous. Take a look around. Do you not see the men looking at you? Right now, they're thinking I'm the luckiest man in this casino."

She smiled, "Luckiest? That's the best you got?"

He shrugged. "If the shoe fits."

"Be careful," she retorted. "It maybe you that a house falls on next."

"Can't hurt the scarecrow. No brains. All stuffing."

"Oh, you! Go get me a drink. I need it."

"And leave you here alone? I may have no brains, but I'm not that stupid."

Lucky's banter had her feeling more relaxed, and the anxiety she felt over seeing A.J. again had lessened. Lucky was right. She needed to confront him. If only for closure. They reached the bar, and Lucky ordered drinks for them both, and they sat there, playing automated poker. Every now and then, Carly took a casual look around the casino floor, wondering when A.J. would show.

She was engrossed in a game with Lucky when she felt someone come up behind her. She tensed, knowing what was about to happen. She reached out and placed a hand on Lucky's leg, just above his knee. Lucky turned and looked at her and smiled, cocking an eyebrow as if to say, "Game on."

"Carly! Is that you?" A.J. exclaimed.

Carly resisted the urge to roll her eyes. They had been engaged and lived together, for Christ's sake. Now he didn't think he recognized her?

"Yes."

"What are you doing here?" he asked.

"Well, you see, Carly here agreed to marry me, and we're here to celebrate our engagement," Lucky said, pulling her close to him. She giggled, leaning into him and playing along.

"That's, that's..." A.J. stammered. "Wow."

"I have to tell you, I am so lucky to find a woman like her." He leaned in and placed a kiss on the top of her head. "How someone could let her go is beyond me." His voice deepened as he said the words, leaving Carly a little breathless and confused.

A.J. had the grace to look chagrined for a moment. "She is quite the woman." He nodded to them. "Best wishes to both of you." He looked at Carly. "You deserve every bit of happiness. Have a good evening. And be sure to go visit the members' desk. The hotel will have something for you to celebrate."

Carly didn't know how her mouth didn't drop open. She was so speechless she was thankful when Lucky responded, "Thank you."

"Enjoy the rest of your evening," he said before turning and disappearing into the crowd.

"What the hell was that?" Carly hissed.

"Looks like the jerk you've hated all this time may actually be human after all."

"He can't be human."

"Why not?"

"Because then..."

"Because then you'd have to let go of that anger?"

She narrowed her eyes at him. "Hush."

He pulled her close in a hug. "Come on, *cher*, let's wander over and see what goodies we have waiting for us. I call dibs if it's a spa day. It's been forever since I had a good pedicure."

Carly rolled her eyes and shook her head at him.

The prize turned out to be a gift certificate at the fancy steakhouse in the casino. Carly's eyes widened when she saw the amount. It would be enough to feed all four of them and then some. Ryder and Julien would be joining them soon. Ryder was cleaning up after work, and Julien had left later than Carly and Lucky had.

She showed the certificate to Lucky, who grinned. "Oh, *cher*. We're going to have fun tonight." He reached down, grabbed her hand, and twirled her in a little circle. "Biloxi looks good on you, girl."

Chapter Twenty-Eight

CARLY SAT ON THE BEACH, watching the sun rise. The peach, pink, and lavender colors were a calming contrast to what was going on inside her head. Seeing A.J. last night, Lucky's attention. Ryder's eyes narrowing as he watched the two of them as they ate dinner.

Her stomach churned as she thought of her affection for Joey and her attraction to Lucky.

Her journal lay open on her lap, but she had yet to write a word. So much for a weekend writing getaway. No way she could write now. Not the way she was feeling. She closed it and set it beside her.

She leaned forward and crossed her arms over her knees, pulling them close. She rested her chin on her knees and stared out at the water. The water gently lapped against the sand as the gulls circled overhead.

Footsteps crunching on the sand caught her attention, and she looked up to see a blonde woman walking up to her.

"Good morning," the woman said, her smile bright.

"Morning," Carly replied.

The woman nodded toward her journal. "Writing this morning?"

"Trying to." Carly shrugged. "Just doesn't seem to be happening."

"Now, that seems to be a problem." The woman plopped down beside Carly. "I'm Penny. I'm a retired journalist. I know all about writer's block. Is there anything I can do to help?"

"I'm Carly. I don't think my stuff is exactly journalism worthy."

"It's still writing. I'm a complete stranger to you, completely unbiased. Why don't you tell me what you what to write about?"

"I want to write about something real."

"Okay. What is real?"

"Love."

Penny laughed, throwing her head back, her blonde hair reflecting the colors of the sunrise. "I don't mean to laugh. Love is real, and it took me a long time to realize that. Now you have me very intrigued. Keep talking."

Carly blurted, "This all started with a pair of shoes."

Penny snickered again. "Oh, girl, we have some stuff in common."

"I've wanted to be a writer for so long, but what I'm writing doesn't have any substance. But today, I keep coming back to this scene with red high heels. It all starts with the shoes."

"Carly, I don't know much about you, but I will tell you this. My love story began anew with a pair of red high heels. I decided to embrace the love I had run from many years ago. I showed up at his house unexpectedly, wearing fabulous shoes. It was tough at first, but now, I'm so happy. He's everything I ever wanted. Do not discount the power of the perfect pair of shoes. And a woman's determination to make it work."

Carly nodded. "That is so awesome!"

Penny stood. "If you ever finish that novel, let me know. I'd love to read it."

"I already have the first line. It all started with a pair of red shoes."

"Perfect. I'm so happy to have met you."

"Me too."

"I'm going to head out. By now, Alex will be ready to go have coffee at Dru's."

"Enjoy. I think I know what I'm going to be doing."

"Glad I could help." With that, she headed off down the beach. Carly picked up her journal and pen. She wrote *It all started with a red pair of shoes...*

She went back to what she had written about Gypsy and started weaving the story together.

She grabbed the keys to her ancient VW bug convertible. She tossed a worn-out suitcase onto the back seat and hopped in. She started the car and backed out of the driveway. Destination? Unknown.

She was free.

She longed to see the stars on the ocean while she sat beside a warm fire. Just her and her guitar.

A gypsy soul, her grandmother had said. But Grannie was gone, her body free from the disease that had taken her life. Grannie's last words to her had been, "Be free, Gypsy. Go see everything I wanted to see. Write your songs. I don't have a lot of money, but what I have is yours."

The wind from the highway dried the tears as they fell. As she crossed the bridge that led out of town, she pulled over. She grabbed those hideous shoes out of the passenger seat, those shoes that symbolized the end of her marriage. She leaned back in a pitcher's pose and chucked those shoes out into the bay. She watched as they sank into the blue depths of the water.

"We're free Grannie. We're finally free."

Carly closed the journal and loaded her things into her backpack. It was time to go see Lucky and make some decisions.

• • • •

"COME IN," LUCKY SAID, motioning her into the hotel room. "Julien went down for some breakfast."

She smiled at him, all rumpled from sleep, and her eyes darted to the messy bed that was probably still warm. Her heart skipped a beat, and those darned butterflies were back. She looked away toward the window to focus.

"What is it, *cher?*" he asked, leaning against the entertainment center, his bare feet crossed.

"Kiss me," she blurted.

His eyes widened. "Excuse me?"

"You heard me. Kiss me."

"I can't just kiss you on demand. Now I'm all awkward." He flashed a dimpled smile.

"Fine, then." She crossed the few steps that separated them. Standing toe to toe with him, she leaned up and looked into his eyes. After one moment of uncertainty, she leaned up and pressed her lips to his. He may have been surprised to begin with, but as soon as their mouths met, he warmed up. He wrapped his hands around her waist and pulled her close to him. Her pulse pounded as she felt his hard chest against her. His kiss was slow, steady, and meant to seduce.

Except for one thing.

He wasn't Joey.

There were butterflies, yes, but not that lightning flash that danced across her body. Not that feeling of coming home that she felt in Joey's arms.

She stopped, took a step back, and smiled at Lucky. She reached up and cupped his cheek.

He faked a smile. "Joey is going to be one very happy man."

"I'm sorry, Lucky."

"*Cher,* don't be. I have enjoyed every moment with you. Besides, you know us LeBlanc men. We're not meant to settle down, anyway."

"I am so glad you came into my life. You have taught me so much."

"I'm happy for that. I will always be here for you, Carly." He pulled her close for a hug, releasing her after a deep breath.

"Wanna have some breakfast?" Carly asked.

"That sounds like a good plan to me. Then how about we call that cousin of mine and see what he's up to today?"

"Perfect. I'm in."

Chapter Twenty-Nine

CARLY PULLED INTO WHAT used to be the parking lot for Snapper's. The entire lot was empty now. The demolition crew had been through and leveled the place and hauled off the debris. It was a fresh slate. The property was ready for a new idea.

But it wouldn't be Carly's new idea.

She walked around the perimeter of the property and stood where she thought the bar had been. She pictured the Saturday regulars and wondered where they went now. Probably back to the Wild Wahoo down the road. She would have to stop in and see.

The kitchen area was next. She remembered the times she had gone in and moved Joey's stuff around when he wasn't looking. How he would swat her with a kitchen towel and run her out. She wondered if he would now. She wasn't the same kitchen idiot she had been only a few weeks ago. She was no Emeril Lagasse, but she could boil water and cook stuff in it.

Continuing to wander, she found herself where she thought the pool table had been. She plopped down cross-legged and tucked a bottle of water by her side. There was no jukebox to play, only the sounds of the occasional passing car on the main road and the sea birds calling overhead.

She rested her elbows on her knees and placed her chin on her folded hands. So much had changed since the night she had seen Jack. The hurricane that had ripped through Bon Chance had not only changed Snapper's; it had changed her.

Ben, I got stuck when you died. The only way I knew how to cope was by keeping this place open for you. But it seems life has a funny way of shaking us up sometimes. I hope you're proud of me. I have a new life now. And I like it.

She sniffed and brushed a tear away. She looked up at the sky and took a deep breath. *I miss you, little brother. We all do. Someday, I will find a new place to hang our picture. I promise. But first, I have a few things I need to do.*

She wiped her tears and reached for the phone in her back pocket. It was time to text Joey.

She hit "send" and went to retrieve the bag and cooler out of her truck. Smiling, she made her way down to the docks, kicked her flip flops off before sitting on the ledge, and waited.

It wasn't long before she heard the sound of footsteps approaching. She turned to see Joey. His dimpled grin made her heart skip a beat.

"Come see," she said, patting the area beside her. She pulled two mason jars out of the bag and the Boone's Farm out of the cooler. She poured them both drinks.

"Brought out the fine stuff today, I see. Should I be scared?" he asked.

"No, I think we're both done with fear."

"Oh?"

She took a breath and looked out over the water. It was a quiet day, not many boats out, so the water was still and calm. Nothing like the chaos going on in her head.

"I don't want to come back here," she said. "Not now. I'm happy in Lafayette. I like working for Emily. And I really like that I've found a circle of writing friends."

He nodded but stayed silent.

She took a sip of her wine before continuing. "Plus, I'm happy doing things on my own now. I don't want to lose that." She reached for his hand, "But I don't want to lose you either."

"What does that mean?" he asked.

"I've been scared for so long, Joey. Of so many things. I'm not anymore." She grinned. "Well, maybe a little."

He laughed, squeezing her hand. She turned slightly so she was facing him.

"I want to see where this can go. Lafayette and New Orleans aren't that far away. I can spend some time there, and you can come explore Lafayette with me too."

He reached out and brushed a strand of hair behind her ear, leaving his palm on her cheek. "I think that sounds perfect."

"You think so?"

"I know so." He leaned in and brushed his lips across hers. The kiss was soft, an exploration of old feelings and new beginnings. He leaned back, cradling her face with his hands. "Welcome home, Carly."

He was right. For her, Joey was home.

Chapter Thirty

TWO MONTHS LATER...

New Orleans

"That guy creeps me out," Lucky said as Alcide, the hotel's head of security, walked in. He was clad in a black suit that looked as if it cost as much as Lucky's land, cabin included. His white shirt was crisp, the collar open. A white handkerchief was folded into his front pocket. Even in his flat-heeled expensive shoes, he stood taller than Lucky.

He walked in as if he owned the place, and Lucky wondered if he did. He reminded Lucky of the song *Sympathy for the Devil.* Alcide was a man of wealth and taste, and Lucky had sympathy for any man, devil, or angel who would tangle with him.

"Yeah, I wouldn't want to meet up with him on one of these side streets alone," Ryder said. That said a lot, considering the amount of bar fights Ryder had engaged in.

Alcide took a glass from the bartender then approached them. "Gentlemen, how are you faring this evening?" His voice was deep and slightly accented.

"We are good," Lucky said. "We're about to head to the ballroom."

"I trust you will have a fine evening. Our social director, Chloe, has spent much time planning."

"I'm sure we will, thank you."

"Now, if you will excuse me." He bowed his head slightly and walked over to a couple seated at the corner of the bar, also clad in evening attire, a dark haired woman, and a man who looked strangely familiar.

"You ready?" Ryder asked. "Joey should be heading down here any time to meet Carly. Let's let them have their moment."

Lucky's heart sank in his chest. He had no desire to see the moment Carly came in and walked into the arms of another man. That loss still stung. He downed his beer and set it on the counter. He slung his arm around Ryder's shoulder. "C'mon, cousin. Let's go see what trouble we can get into."

As Ryder and Lucky walked into the lobby, they met Grace and Gabriel, who had come in for the holidays. Even in formal wear, Grace still looked like the rocker she was. She wore her dark hair straight. Fingerless black leather gloves adorned her arms, and the banding around the straps of her black gown was covered in black studs. As she saw them, she held up two fingers in the classic rock greeting.

"You are stunning," Ryder said, leaning in to kiss her cheek. Lucky had to agree. They had met the couple for drinks the night before, and Lucky had admired her attitude.

"Thank you," she said, turning a bit to show off her dress. Ryder took a moment to do the introductions, then Grace said, "Are you all ready to head in there? I still can't believe Carly talked me into this."

"You know Carly." Ryder pointed out his tuxedo. "Do you really think I want to be here?"

Grace laughed. "Not at all." She linked her arm in his. "Come on. Behave, and I'll let you spin me around the dance floor a time or two."

"Now you're talking."

• • • •

JOEY STOOD AT THE BAR in the lounge area of the Chateau Rouge. He couldn't wait to see Carly.

"You look like you're about to jump out of your skin."

Joey started when the bartender took a seat next to him. She took a sip from her wineglass etched with the phrase "Blood of my Enemies." Joey looked at her, with her steely gray eyes filled with mischief and menace. If anyone had the blood of their enemies in a glass, it would be Ivy.

Clad in a red and black evening gown, her hair a wild mass of raven curls, she had the attention of everyone in the room. Judging by the sly smile she wore, she was quite aware of that fact.

"I was just chatting with your friends Ryder and Lucky. They are quite the charmers. They're looking quite tasty in those tuxes."

The way she drew out the word "tasty" sent a chill up Joey's spine. There was something about this woman that unnerved him. He couldn't quite put his finger on it.

He only knew he was glad she hadn't turned her attention to him.

She winked. "Yet."

Joey's eyes widened. Before he could recover, she slid out of the seat. "I believe the woman you're waiting for is about to enter."

How would she know? He gulped his beer, hoping to steel his nerves. Ivy and the wait for Carly were making him half crazy.

He looked at the time on his phone. She was ten minutes late. Had she changed her mind? His heart beat hard in his chest. Had this all been for nothing?

She walked through the doorway, and Joey stopped breathing.

Her deep red velvet dress hugged her curves. The V of the neckline exposed just enough skin to make his mouth go dry. She wore a black lace masquerade mask that covered the top part of her face, emphasizing her dark red lips. Her blonde hair spilled over her shoulders in soft, sexy waves.

She smiled when she saw him before walking over to him with a grace he had never seen from her before.

She did a spin when she reached him. "What do you think?"

He shook his head. "I'm speechless."

She grinned as he pulled her close. He breathed in the smell of her hair, his body reacting to the citrus scent and the feel of her body pressed to his. He couldn't wait to dance with her. To feel her sway to the rhythm of the music, like they used to do before life went sideways.

Her heard her sigh as he hugged her closer, as if she felt the same.

"I've missed you," she said as she pulled back so she could look him in the eyes.

"Oh, baby. I've missed you too." He hugged her again, this time kissing the top of her head. "You look absolutely breathtaking tonight, by the way."

"Thank you. You look awesome too. All this for me?"

"Anything for you, Carly. Anything."

She looked up at him again, her eyes expectant. He lowered his lips to hers, and with a restraint he didn't know he had, kissed her slowly, relishing the feel of her full, soft lips against his.

Reluctantly, he pulled back. He ran his hands up her arms to her bare shoulders. "Are you ready, Princess Carly?"

"Lead the way, my prince. And by the way," she teased, "it's Queen Carly."

He laughed and held out the crook of his arm, and she promptly tucked her hand in the curve. "Your chariot awaits."

Two formally clad bellmen, white gloves and all, flanked the double-doored entry to the ballroom. They nodded then opened the carved doors in unison.

"Ready?" Joey asked.

"More than ready. Look at this! The Chateau Rouge doesn't play when it comes to throwing a party. This may put Jay Gatsby to shame."

"Shall we promenade?"

"Yes, we shall."

They stepped into the huge room, and Carly gasped. The room was done in tones of red, gold, and black. Christmas trees adorned with tiny twinkling crystal lights lined the walls. The white linen adorned tables were dotted with centerpieces with red roses and gold masquerade masks.

She searched the crowd of partygoers, some wearing masks, some not, for their friends. She finally spotted Lucky and Ryder standing near the bar. Of course.

She nodded to Joey, who had spotted them also. They made their way through the crowd to meet them. Carly was thrilled to see Grace and Gabriel were there too. If only Noah and Emily had chosen to come. But she had completely understood.

Grace looked like she could kick someone's ass then get up on the stage and sing a song about it. "You look awesome, Grace," Carly said as she hugged her.

"You too."

"Isn't this incredible?" Carly asked, looking around the room.

"It's amazing."

"Not as amazing as you two," Gabriel said, leaning in to give Carly a peck on the cheek.

"Aw, you're looking good yourself, Gabe."

Ryder rolled his eyes. "Come on, now, we all look hot, if I do say so myself."

"Of course you do," Carly said. She looked at Lucky, who was stunning in evening wear, albeit a little uncomfortable.

He smiled in greeting, but his eyes were shadowed. "Hello, Carly. You're looking good."

"You too. Two good-looking LeBlanc men? This room is in trouble. Don't go breaking too many hearts."

The lights went out, pitching the room into darkness lit only by the candles on the tables.

A spotlight flashed on, highlighting Ivy on the stage. She looked just as she had in the bar earlier, only this time, she had red and black feathers adorning her hair.

Behind her, a small jazz band began to play the beginning sounds of *Baby It's Cold Outside*.

"Is that...?"

"The bartender? Yes."

"No, I mean the guy."

"It can't be. He supposedly died from a brain tumor last year."

"Must be someone who looks a lot like him."

"It's uncanny, really."

As Ivy began to sing, the crowd went silent. She sang with an old-world sound that reminded Carly of Ella Fitzgerald. She swayed slightly to the music and smiled. The entire room fell under her spell.

"Ladies and gentlemen, let's give a big round of applause to Ivy and her singing partner."

The woman standing on the stage waited for the sound to die down before continuing. "My name is Chloe Devereaux, and I would like to formally welcome you to the first annual Christmas masquerade ball here at the Chateau Rouge. We hope you all have a wonderful and enchanting evening. Now, if you will, please welcome our entertainment for the night, Leauxco."

The band took the stage. "Welcome everyone," the lead singer said. "We're the band Leauxco from Baton Rouge, and we're so happy to be here performing tonight. We're going to start off with an original song. I hope you all like it."

It was a fast-moving song that had the group out on the dance floor. As Carly heard the chorus, she pulled Joey close and kissed him. The rest of the room seemed to disappear as he wrapped his arms around her and held her close as he returned the embrace.

She leaned into to him, loving the feel of his warmth. His strength. He was her rock. Her knight in shining armor. Her happily ever after.

• • • •

"BUT HOW CLOSE IS TOO close
And how much is too much
How much can I say before you run away
And I lose it all
How hard must I try
To put my dreams aside
And open your eyes so you'll realize
Once and for all
That the fear, the fear is worse than the fall..."

Epilogue

CARLY INHALED A DEEP breath as she rolled the wagon full of signing stuff into the market area. It was quiet, as she was the first to arrive. As she walked up, Gwen, the manager, came to meet her.

"Carly, it's so good to see you again. You're going to be in booth three." She took a moment to show Carly the outlets and give general directions. "The bar will open soon, and you can have a drink while you wait."

"I could definitely use one of those," she said, laughing. Her stomach had been in knots all day. Her first big signing. She'd practiced her name, her pitch, and everything she could think of. She'd even done a mock-up table setup to see how her book would look. Yet, even as she pulled the table out of the wagon, she noticed her hands were trembling.

A few minutes later, she was putting the finishing touches on her table, after rearranging it for the third time. She took one last look at it then sat in the folding chair behind the table. In a few hours, this place would be full of people.

She looked at the bar, and it still seemed closed, so she grabbed her phone and scrolled through social media to keep her mind occupied.

Joey: I'm half an hour away.
Carly: Be careful. But hurry. I'm nervous.
Joey: You're going to be fine.

The bartender arrived, and she ordered a drink to take the edge off. In an hour, she would be doing her first book event since *Gypsy Soul* had been published. She had practiced her pitch all morning in the mirror. She had run it by Gibson over coffee until she felt she wouldn't get tongue-tied when she was asked what her book was about.

Dawn arrived next, and Carly all but dragged her to where she had set up her books.

"It looks great, Carly. It really does. That cover is awesome too." Dawn smiled. "And just wait until you have more than one book and have to figure out how to place them."

"I can't even think about that yet," Carly said. "I feel overwhelmed now as it is."

"You'll get there. Come on, let's go finish our drinks and relax. It's a gorgeous evening, and the crowd should be good. Oh, and Dylan's on his way. He's running late."

Carly laughed. "I am not surprised."

Joey arrived next, greeting her with a big hug and a kiss. He had ended up taking a job he couldn't resist in the French Quarter, and they split their weekends between New Orleans and Lafayette now that Carly and Emily had become partners in the Cypress Café.

She truly had the best of both worlds.

Later, the line of people streamed by her table, many stopping by to ask about her book, her journey, or just to give her a word of encouragement. Several stopped and bought books. After a few drinks and a few spiels, Carly had relaxed and had actually started to enjoy herself.

As the crowd slowed down, Carly had time to take a breath. Looking over at Joey, who sat at the bar, she smiled when he caught her eye. Her smile grew as he winked.

She looked at her group of friends, both old and new. Watched as they laughed among themselves, all here for her.

She raised her eyes to the sky, looking out at the wide expanse of sparkling stars. This was exactly where she was supposed to be.

Once and for all, the fear was worse than the fall.

A Note to Readers

DEAR READER,

Thank you so much for reading *Once and for All*. I hope you enjoyed reading it as much as I did writing it. Even though Carly did drive me nuts at times. Here are some fun facts about this book and the series in general.

- This book took me three years to write. I had a few distractions along the way, and every time I did work on it, I couldn't figure out where it was going. I think it's because Carly hadn't decided either.
- All the dogs in this novel are either dogs that have owned me or are my reader's pets. Chance, Sammy, and Oscar have all been mine.
- If you've read the first two books in this series, you know that Kevin Douglas has been considering running against the corrupt Moutons in Pointe Shade. We will see the outcome of this in "Wishing on a Christmas Star" a fourth book in the Boonie series that will be released later.
- All is not lost with Snapper's Bar and Grill either, if you haven't read "Saving Grace" in the *Finally Home* anthology, you will see which of the Boonies decide to rebuild. You may be surprised. Click on the link for more information about Finally Home.

https://amzn.to/2zUtxXw

- There are three more Boonie books in the works.

These will feature three men who appear in this book.

- The Chateau Rouge in New Orleans is actually the fictional hotel in which my Jolie St. Amant stories take place. It's always fun to have the Boonies make an appearance in these crossovers.
- Want to learn how to make a gumbo? Check out the Real Cajun Recipes site:

https://bit.ly/3iraDrL

Bon Chance!
A.L. Vincent

Tangled up in You

Sign up for my newsletter for information on future Bon Chance Boonie Books!

http://eepurl.com/bRiinr

Acknowledgements

A BIG THANK YOU TO Neil Ray and Leauxco for providing the inspiration for the title of this book and allowing me to use some of the lyrics. It was such a beautiful fit for the story.

As always, many thanks to my Boonies! Your support has meant the world to me and keeps me going when the writing life gets tough.

Lori, in only one edit, I've already learned so much about my own craft and how I can tweak it to make it better.

The gorgeous cover designed by Ashley may be my favorite yet. And considering the brilliant covers you've already done, that's saying so much.

Thanks to my weekend writing group, Dennis, Connie, and Alex for helping me work out the bugs in the beginning.

And to my readers, thank you for being a part of Carly's journey! It was a long one, but her story is finished, once and for all....

Don't miss out!

Visit the website below and you can sign up to receive emails whenever A. L. Vincent publishes a new book. There's no charge and no obligation.

https://books2read.com/r/B-A-FJAK-JIXHB

BOOKS 2 READ

Connecting independent readers to independent writers.

Also by A. L. Vincent

Bon Chance Boonies
Once and For All

BIENVENUE PRESS

About the Publisher

Bienvenue Press opened its doors in June 2017. While our initial focus is on Southern fiction, we hope to branch out into other genres in the future as we continue to grow. In order to help our authors make their books the best they can be, we plan to publish six books in our inaugural year.

Our staff has years of combined experience in the writing and editing world. We are teachers, writers, journalists, and readers. We have a deep love for words, writing, and books.

Join our reader's group to stay updated on new releases! https://bit.ly/2OFOM46